Disabling Relics for Dummies

JB TREPAGNIER

Map art by Abdur Roub

Illustrations by Nancy Afroditae

Cover art by Hannah Stern-Jakob Designs

❀ Created with Vellum

The Profane World

THE MUSEUM OF THE PROFANE

THE ACADEMY OF THE PROFANE

THE LIBRARY OF THE PROFANE

THE PROFANE WORLD

I was back in my cottage on the museum grounds after everything that happened in Hell with my sister. I didn't regret going. I'd follow my twin anywhere, especially if she were in danger. I got to see history unfold. I met my fucking creator, *and* she programmed her number into my phone to keep in touch. I thought she was just taking the piss with all of us, but she texted me the next morning to see if everything was okay at the museum while I was gone and warned me to be careful with the shipment from the Cult of the Aether Sisters like this big god mama bear.

I lost my shit when I woke up and saw that. I had a pretty good idea what Ripley was up to, but I called her anyway. Your twin sister was the only person on the planet where it was acceptable to cock block you when you were probably having an orgy. I was also the only person alive Ripley would answer the phone for when she was getting dicked stupid.

Unless she was past the point of no return, in which case, she'd call me right back.

After getting an entire rant about some kid named

Dennis, her desk, and the state of her library, Ripley told me she got a text, too. We both kind of lost our shit for a bit.

My museum wasn't in the same state as Ripley's library because I had help. I ran the museum and handled anything dangerous that came in, but I had a team at my back. Some of these people had been here forever, and some I hired. Ripley *should* have had that at the library.

The Library of the Profane was massive, and I always said she needed help. There probably should have been an entire person dedicated to that vault of books that had attacked my sister more than once, but I seemed to think that more than she did.

Focusing on my sister and what happened in Hell let me keep my mind off the total shitshow that was my life. Valentine showed up at my museum right when I first got hired and totally played me. That never happened to me before. I usually caught on quickly and ended it before I got hurt.

He said *everything* right. He brought relics from a dig to my museum and had all sorts of fascinating things to say about them. Valentine was a total beast in bed. I thought he was the one, even though Ripley was like a little devil on my shoulder telling me to run because he couldn't tell us apart. We might be identical and have the same taste in clothes, but we wore our hair and makeup differently.

Ripley spent a lot of time and money to make our curly hair look good. I didn't want to deal with hair that would betray me whenever the weather went wonky. So I *always* straightened my curls. It wasn't just our hair. We had completely different piercings and tattoos. Fuck. I had a signature black lipstick I'd been wearing since the academy that was a dead giveaway, I wasn't my twin sister.

I made excuses like an idiot. He kept asking me to get his books in the Library of the Profane. I gave them to my sister, and she told me not only were they terrible, but he was definitely a serial cheater. I was convinced it would be different for me.

He had to leave to go on a dig. I went dick stupid. Valentine stopped messaging and calling. When his dig ended, he didn't immediately come back. He sent me a signed copy of the book he wrote while he was gone. It was pretty much chock full of all his sexual experiences while he was away.

I was devastated and swore off men. Now he was coming back.

I know Ripley and Killian thought I dyed my hair red because I wanted him back. I didn't. I wanted him to know damned sure who I was when Ripley and I were in the same room because I was planning something. I didn't know what the fuck that was just yet, but it was going to be epic. *No one* played me like that and got away with it.

"Tea?" Killian said, sliding my favorite over.

That was another thing I was avoiding. Killian showed up in my life about two hours before Felix came to my sister. He knew everything about me. I was just as close to Killian as I was to Ripley. After we graduated and got our jobs at the museum and library, we weren't roommates anymore, but Killian and I were.

Bats were a little different to take care of than cats. I was going through a little goth phase when Killian showed up and was super excited my familiar ended up a bat. I learned everything I could about taking care of him and found a vet that could care for him in case anything happened.

Then, Reyson happened.

I saw how Felix and Ripley were after Reyson gave Felix his body back. So when I asked Killian if he wanted Reyson to do the same, I wasn't even thinking about that. All my stupid lizard brain was thinking about was the fact that Killian was my best friend, and now that the option was available, the choice should be his.

Now, he was here, with his sandy blond hair always in his eyes and those ridiculous spectacles he wore the last time he was alive. He was the living embodiment of the deathly hot nerd, and he was brilliant to boot. Killian was better than any man I'd ever dated before, and I was too scared to even kiss him.

I'd honestly never been in this situation before. If I was into someone, I told them. I just couldn't do that with Killian. What if he didn't feel the same? What if he did, and I totally fucked this up? Would that be better or worse than how things were now?

Killian pushed his glasses up his nose and squinted at the clock in the kitchen. He conjured the same glasses he wore when he died, when Reyson gave him his body back. I'd already hired him as my research assistant, so he had money and wasn't dependent on me for everything. He was a proud warlock, and I *needed* him to help me.

Still, I'd noticed him squinting a lot when we researched the Cult of the Aether Sisters. There was a lot I *wasn't* saying when I usually told him everything, but I would do something about this.

"Get dressed. We're going to get you an eye exam and better glasses. I know you can't see well. You should have said something."

He gave me this look like he knew damned well there were things I needed to say too, but he wasn't saying them either. Fuck, we were such a pair, and when he was still a bat, he gave me opinions on sexy underwear. Now, I couldn't even tell him how I felt.

"We were kind of busy with Dorian Gray drama," he tossed over his shoulder.

That fucker. I kind of wished Reyson would bring him back to life so I could break his face again. I just *could not* hit him enough.

Can I say how much I adored Killian's fashion sense now that he had his body back? I heard him and Felix talk. Killian had died right around the time Felix was born. Killian came from a prominent witch line in London, and I was certain he dressed super fancy.

He went for total comfort now. He had his favorite bands since he became my familiar. He wore band tees and baggy jeans with chains or a big comfy hoodie if it was chilly out. I avoided telling him he looked sexy or even checking him out as we went out to my car.

What in the world was happening to me? I intended to use every feminine wile at my disposal to get back at Valentine when he got here, and I couldn't even bring myself to flirt with Killian.

CHAPTER 2

Ravyn

The supernatural community liked to pretend we were above mass consumerism and shopping malls, but that was just a lie we told ourselves when we wanted to feel superior to humans. Honestly, we loved spending money just as much as humans did. We just didn't build sprawling shopping malls that a human would wander in to check out and wonder why there was no Macys and food court.

But there were certain areas full of businesses that only catered to the supernatural. I'd already taken Killian there to buy clothes and a blank grimoire so he could start rebuilding his. If I had known he was having trouble seeing then, we would have made another stop.

Killian was being Killian and trying to put me at ease. He turned the radio up and started dancing in his seat.

"We should hit up the food cart run by those Pakistani shifters."

"Ooh, good idea," I said.

There were all kinds of food carts and sit-down places in

the supernatural market. Ripley had her hands full with Reyson and Felix's bromance over modern snacks. Killian couldn't pull whatever he wanted out of thin air like Reyson could, but I had a little monster who was interested in all the foods that wasn't available the last time he was alive.

I found a parking spot, and we went to the optometrist. Eye exams were much different for us than they were for humans.

"You don't have to stay with me for the exam, Ravyn. Can you pick me up some potion ingredients? I'm trying to build up supplies, and I don't want to dip into yours."

I slid one of my credit cards over to him since he hadn't been paid yet at the museum.

"Use this to pay for the exam and new glasses. You're going to need crystals, black salt, and candles. You'll want to pick out your altar and offering items yourself, but I can stock everything else."

"Go forth and shop, young Jedi. I trust you with my supplies."

I wasn't going to go overboard, assuming what he needed. He taught me everything he knew, but I wasn't going to assume what kind of potions he'd regularly make now that he was able. Still, most witches with decent parents got little witchy care packages when their powers awakened with the basics.

Ooh! I didn't just need to put one together for Killian. Little Beyla was fucking adorable and only just found out she was a witch. Kaine moved her to a high school for supernaturals, but all her classmates would be without her magic. All they'd be teaching her was our history, the *theory* behind magic, but not actually how to use what was currently flowing through her veins.

I was totally making her a witchy care package.

There were two shops here I loved for stocking up on

supplies, and I hit up both of them. I was in there long enough for Killian to finish his exam and get his new glasses. But when I got back to where he was supposed to be, he was missing.

He didn't have a cell phone yet, and I didn't have any supplies to do a tracking spell in the middle of the market. So where the hell did my familiar disappear to with my credit card? I didn't know his spending habits now that he had his body back and this market had anything your black heart desired.

"Ravyn? That's way more than I need."

I whirled around, and Killian was standing there with new glasses and a small bag. Okay, he was wearing thick, black hipster glasses and looked sexy as fuck. I tried to hide it, but I totally sexually objectified him in my head long enough for him to notice. He smirked at me, but he didn't say a word about it.

"I got supplies for Beyla, too. I think Kaine is going to make a great protective adoptive daddy for her, and no one is going to hurt her like that again, but he's not a witch."

"Good idea. Word of advice. You saw his dragon in action in Hell. I'd avoid corrupting that girl. So, I adore your new hair. I have my body back in a new century and want to do things totally different from the last time I was alive. Will you put green streaks in my hair?"

Was Killian literally trying to murder me? I was already constantly trying to keep my eyes off of him. Green streaks in his hair? Just kill me now. One of my weaknesses had always been men who just didn't care what people thought about them and did what they wanted. I *totally* got what my sister saw in Balthazar.

Yeah, big sexy Alphas who all looked and acted the same were fun, but I never really wanted to keep one longer than a day. Valentine was the one exception to that.

I'd put the green streaks in his hair. I'd do anything he

asked. I'd just been avoiding touching him in any way because I thought I'd say something stupid and offend him.

I didn't know if he felt the same, and I was actually fucking terrified to find out.

Ravyn was perfect. I mean, she had her flaws. We all did. Hers just meshed well with mine. They paired us up for a reason. It was an honor to be called as a witch's familiar, but I would admit to having a lot of reservations at first. It had been a long time since I walked the Earth. I didn't know what things were like anymore. I didn't know what people were like.

I loved this century. I loved that Ravyn could study what she wanted, wear what she wanted, and give her opinions when no one really asked her. The humans would have burned her alive back in my day, and the supernatural community wasn't much better when it came to the treatment of women.

Not only did Ravyn not have to live by the rules of my day, but neither did I. I hadn't really thought about that until Reyson came into the picture. This was my second chance, and I didn't intend to do a damned thing the same.

I wasn't going to dress in stupid clothes I hated that were uncomfortable because that's what they expected of a warlock of my station. I followed all the stifling rules of the aristocracy

11

the last time I was alive because there weren't really any other options. I had those now.

There were also rules about who you could fall in love with. Most of the time, rich men sold their daughters to richer men for land, titles, and money, and everyone just went with that. Divorce was an option for men by the time I was born, but not for any woman who was being mistreated.

I already knew who I wanted. She was gorgeous, brilliant, and fate already paired us together. I would never press her, but I saw how she stared at me when she thought I didn't notice. I understood why she hadn't said anything, even though she always did when she was into someone.

His name was Valentine, and his stupid mutton chops were about to come back into Ravyn's life. Ravyn liked a pretty face, but she got bored fast if the only topic a person could talk about was themselves. That was all that plonker did, but he traveled around the world digging up dangerous relics, so there was an entertaining spin to it.

He broke her heart, and she entered into a committed relationship with her vibrator after that. She ran wingman for Ripley when they went out, but she shut anyone down who approached her. I *knew* what I'd be up against as soon as Reyson offered to give me my body back.

Then, fucking Valentine called that Gertrude Von Stein signed and contract with him to come back, and now she was a redhead.

I wasn't going to stoop to his level. I wasn't going to kick the door in with this big show of machismo, telling her exactly what she wanted to hear, and then disappearing like he did. I had scruples.

But I was enjoying her hands in my hair as she put the green streaks in it. She put a cap over my hair, and now we were just waiting.

"Do you think it's too much to paint my fingernails?" I asked.

Was it? It was unheard of back in my time, but men did it now. I wasn't ready for makeup and glitter like Balthazar. I didn't know if I'd ever be ready for that. But I *was* open-minded and trying to figure out where I fit into this new century. I wanted to paint my fingernails.

"Say no more," Ravyn said, pulling a box off her dresser. "I wouldn't be caught dead in pink nail polish, so all of these are black, blue, green, or purple. Let's do a manicure. What color?"

Was it creepy that I even paid attention to her nail polish when I was a bat? I used to sit on her shoulder while Ravyn did her nails, and we chatted and gossiped. I'd admire her manicure when she was finished, and I *definitely* had a favorite.

"The green one that is so dark, it's practically black."

Ravyn nodded and waved at me.

"Just like our souls. I love it. The longer you leave that dye on, the better. Give me your hands."

Before she could even touch me, and she'd been avoiding doing that until I asked her to do my hair, her cell phone rang. No one from work called her on the weekend. It was usually Ripley or one of her friends. She glanced at it but didn't answer.

"You should get that."

"It's that wolf turd, Valentine, and it's my day off."

That was... new. When he first left, she used to stare at her phone and jump every time it rang, hoping it was him. She picked up right away when he called to say he was coming back. She said some nasty things about him when he left, but not since she knew he was returning.

"What was that about?" I asked.

Before she could answer, the phone started ringing again. I

knew it was him without asking. Ravyn had been at his beck and call before. I imagined most of the women he took up with were. Valentine didn't like being ignored. She just glared at her phone and rolled her eyes. I gave her a look to answer it. The longer she ignored it, the more he was going to call. Then she was just going to get cranky.

"Can I help you?"

She took the phone away from her ear and put it on speaker where I could hear. That was also new. Ravyn's conversations with Valentine were always private, and I left the room when they were together. This witch was up to something. I loved it.

"We had some problems on the ship coming over. We were in the middle of the ocean when all the instruments on the ship just stopped working, and the wind stopped."

"I swear to shit, Valentine, if you bring *another* ghost into my museum, I'm going to murder you."

We *did not* need more ghosts on these grounds. Especially not from deranged coven members that were definitely not witches, but everyone thought they were. We only found out the Cult of the Aether Sisters weren't dark witches when we were in Hell, and Lilith told us they weren't her creation. Some of the ghosts that were already here were miserable assholes.

"I didn't. Doctor Key has been a tremendous asset. He's the world's leading expert on the cult. He did the rites, and he could get the ship running again. Doctor Key is a powerful warlock."

My eyes met Ravyn's, and we both frowned. We'd both been waist-deep in research into the Cult of the Aether sisters, and we'd never come across a Doctor Key. And he couldn't have known the rites if they weren't witches. No one would have known the rites because Ravyn and I didn't know what the fuck they were.

"I haven't come across him in my research," Ravyn said.

"He'll be working with us at the museum when we get there. Trust me. He's full of all sorts of information about the cult. Doctor Key has been a tremendous help."

"What's his first name?" Ravyn asked.

I yanked her laptop into my lap and pulled up a page to search. I trusted this Doctor Key about as far as I could throw him. I didn't really trust anyone closely related to that cult.

"Honestly? I don't know. He gets really upset if you don't call him Doctor."

"Only Doctor Who is allowed to do that," I said.

Valentine cleared his throat.

"You have a man there with you? On your day off? Who is that, Ravyn?"

"That's Killian."

It was stupid to try to hide I had a body now. Felix was pretty open with it. Of course, Valentine didn't even remember the name of her familiar. He went all grumpy fuck she wasn't alone and let out a possessive growl.

"Is that it?" Ravyn asked.

"Yeah, sorry. I just wanted to let you know about the hiccup."

They disconnected, and Ravyn held out her hands to paint my fingernail. Of two things, I was certain. Valentine was trying to rekindle something.

And Ravyn was up to something.

CHAPTER 4

Ravyn

I was in so much trouble. Now that I'd touched Killian, I didn't want to stop. His hair was just so soft. He didn't want to use my Moon Rider scented hair stuff because he said it would be weird. So he picked up a more masculine scented witchy shampoo, and it smelled amazing. And doing his nails? There were just these jolts when our skin made contact.

He had a rocking manicure and washed the dye out of his hair. I was just sitting here so confused, when my phone rang. It had better not be Valentine again. I didn't really need to know about the ship's malfunction. It was probably a damned ghost. I didn't particularly want to deal with deranged cult member ghosts in my museum, but eh. Dangerous relics generally came with shitty spirits attached to them.

I didn't know where Valentine found this Doctor Key, but I'd been researching in the museum archives, online, and in the Library of the Profane, and his name never came up. He hadn't even been quoted. Minerva had been after me to write a book about what I did at the museum like she had with her curses. I hadn't yet, but I'd been quoted in plenty of articles and books by various historians and researchers.

This Key guy? Nothing. He didn't even have a blog. He didn't have a single peer-reviewed paper anywhere online. Who was fact-checking this guy? I was pretty sure he didn't do the proper rites on the cult for those skeletons they found because every single historical document on them was that they were dark witches with bear familiars.

I hadn't questioned that before. No one really did, even when it would be extremely rare for a witch to even call a bear as a familiar. It would be rare for just one witch, much less an entire coven of them. Witches who weren't given familiars by the cosmos sometimes took it personally. They tried all sorts of dark magic to get a familiar. It wasn't possible.

Even if the Cult of the Aether sisters had somehow figured that out, it would have been pretty impossible to force a bear to your will. Plus, I'd met Lilith. She knew her creations better than anyone, and she didn't claim the Cult of the Aether Sisters.

Which meant this mystery warlock *definitely* didn't know the right rites for them. If he was an expert on the cult, people would be clamoring for quotes and interviews. If he wrote a book, it would be a best seller if he did and knew the truth about what they really were. The Cult of the Aether Sisters was wiped out centuries ago, but we still used them as boogeymen for supernatural kids.

Shit, my mom used to tell Ripley and me if we didn't stop complaining about doing the dishes, the ghosts of the cult were going to send their bears to eat us. If you got drunk around a bonfire, *someone* would tell an urban legend about them. They were still pretty famous. Fuck, even if he knew nothing and published total lies, but they were *juicy* lies, people would have bought it.

So, yeah, they were definitely bringing me ghosts. I wasn't

super happy about that, but it wasn't like we didn't have a ton of pissed off ghosts here already.

Killian came out of the bathroom, drying his hair. I was about to tell him he looked good, but my phone rang. It had better not be Valentine again. I looked down, and it was my sister. I'd always pick up for her.

"Did you come up for a breather from all the post Hell dick celebrations?" I asked.

"None of us were blessed with super genitals and needed a breather. Want to come give moral support to a god while a Hellhound pierces his nipples?"

"That's weird, Ripley, even for you."

"Well, *my* nipples aren't pierced, but yours are. Bram's are too, but you can help walk Reyson through it."

"Hold on. Killian, do we want to go watch Bram pierce Reyson's nipples?"

"Are you kidding? That would be thrilling. You saw what he did to Dorian. It's a fifty-fifty chance he's going to get dramatic when Bram shoves a needle in his nipple."

"Good point. We'll be there, but if Reyson randomly decides he wants his dick pierced while we are there, I'm going to need therapy. I'm all about seeing what god dick looks like, but not when it's being used on my twin sister."

"He's not going to whip his cock out in front of my twin sister, Ravyn. He knows I'll kill him for that. Felix would get mad, too. He gets all offended when dicks come out for no reason."

"Do I want to know why dicks are coming out for no reason in your library?"

"Probably not. Get over here."

I hung up and looked over at Killian. He looked amazing with his hair and nails like that. I was trying so hard not to stare, but I'd always been honest with him before. This was all new to him. I got it. He was fully embracing having his body back in this century. He'd always supported me in everything, even if it was a spectacularly stupid idea.

"Damn, son. You look fine as hell like that."

Killian pushed his glasses up his nose and gave me a knowing smirk. Did he feel the same thing I felt when we were touching? He used to tell me not to wear certain trousers out because they made my ass look big. If he could go there with me, he would definitely say something if he felt the same vibes I was, so I changed the subject.

"Let's go watch a god get his nipples pierced."

CHAPTER 5

Killian

I certainly never got invited to these many nipple piercings the last time I was alive. I was there with Ravyn when she got hers done because if someone was going to shove needles through her nipples, they had better be treating her breasts like precious cargo. They were *really* nice breasts.

After Ravyn, I didn't expect to witness another one. Ripley was with us and said she didn't want hers done. Reyson was Reyson, though. Ripley said he wouldn't, but I wouldn't put it past him to decide on a cock piercing while we were there.

He could be this big teddy bear with his fondness for modern junk food and devotion to Ripley, but honestly? He terrified me. I heard the story about how Felix got his body back. Felix knocked over his cookies because he was a cat. Reyson changed his inky black coat to have white fur on his face in the shape of a dick.

Felix was understandably pissed about it, and Ripley asked Reyson to put it back. He didn't want her to be mad at him. So instead of just putting Felix's fur back, he left it the way it was and managed to give him his body back in its prime. Just to impress Ripley because he wanted to marry her.

We all saw what he did to Dorian Gray for kidnapping Ripley. Demon magic was completely unfamiliar to me, but everyone on Earth feared it because if you made a deal, there was no fighting it when payment was due. When those women flung it at Reyson, it destroyed his clothes but didn't leave a mark on him.

I didn't know him nearly as well as Ripley and her guys, but you wouldn't catch me anywhere near his nipples with a sharp needle, even if he asked. I *just* got my body back, and he could be petty.

When we got to Ripley's apartment, apparently, Reyson wasn't the only one getting pierced. Balthazar was running around topless for some reason, but was getting two spikes in his lip. Gabriel wanted a ring at the top of his ear, and Ripley was getting a nostril piercing. I didn't peg Felix for getting anything pierced, but he wanted his ears done.

"Seriously, Ripley? You invited me to your harem piercing party?"

"You went and got new hair. I thought you might want a new piercing, too. Killian has new hair too. He might want something pierced as well. Bram apprenticed at a piercing shop in New York, so he knows what he's doing. He works there sometimes for cash when he's on extended trips here. So he knows what he's doing."

Ravyn might not want something, but did I? I'd been with the twins every time they got a new piercing or tattoo. I talked about the pros and cons with Ravyn when she wanted a new one. I heard her talk about the endorphin rush afterward.

Yeah, I wanted one.

"I think I want my septum pierced."

"That's going to be totally adorable. Don't you think, Ravyn?" Ripley said, giving her a pointed look.

Before I knew it, Bram was preparing Balthazar, Felix had kidnapped me, and Ripley ran off with Ravyn. I knew what this was. This was a divide and conquer, good old fashioned witch intervention disguised as a piercing party. I sat next to Felix in the chair.

"Hit me with it. What's the *real* reason for the invite?"

"Reyson was already planning that piercing, and we joined in. Ripley is worried about her twin. Valentine is coming back, and I think we'd all prefer to see her with you."

So would I.

"You're dating Ripley, Felix. You've been around Ravyn. You know she doesn't do anything she doesn't want to do. Would you and Ripley be together right now if she hadn't aggressively pursued you? Ravyn hasn't done that."

"Yeah, that's true. Ripley has had her heart broken but not totally stomped on how Valentine did Ravyn. Ravyn hasn't dated since then. We can all see how the two of you look at each other."

"I'm not blind, Felix, but I'm not going to rush her either. I'm letting her do this on her own time. She's not running back to Valentine now that he's back. Ravyn is up to something. I'm not sure what, but it's not jumping back in bed with him. She'll tell me that when she's ready too."

"Oh, good. We have revenge mode Ravyn. That's a good sign."

"Minerva Krauss has been after Ravyn to write a book about some of the things she deals with at the museum. If she cracks some of the mysteries behind the Cult of the Aether Sisters when that shipment comes in, it'll put her mark on the entire world. We all know that wouldn't be possible without Valentine. She couldn't exactly tell him not to bring the items to the museum because this is a pretty major find. Gertrude Von Stein was the one who arranged it, anyway. It'll be subtle because it involves work, and Ravyn is a professional, but it's going to happen."

"How do we help?" Felix asked.

"You don't. She hasn't even told me what she's up to. This is Ravyn's fight. Yeah, we all want to castrate Valentine, but we aren't the one he wronged. She has a lot on her plate right now. Even if someone other than Valentine brought those items, this discovery is pretty major. Add to that, her twin sister just got kidnapped and everything that happened in Hell.

"I get that you and Ripley want her happy, and I want that, too. I always have. I'm just saying this is not the time to worry about relationships or playing matchmaker. Valentine called earlier, and something on that ship shut down all the instruments. He's brought in some warlock claiming to be an expert on the cult, but we can't even find a quote from him in any of our research. There's too much going on to worry about that right now."

"You're probably right. Ripley is just so happy, and she wants that for her twin."

"Please tell me she hasn't abducted Ravyn and having a come to Lilith talk about men with her. The twins are close and talk about everything, but they have a long, hallowed tradition of never listening to each other when it comes to men."

"Oh, shit. The last time the twins disagreed on *anything* major was when Ravyn was involved with Valentine for the first time, and Ripley didn't like him. We'd better get in there before it gets ugly."

It rarely got ugly with the twins. They didn't get mad if one of them borrowed the other's clothes without asking. If they were involved with a guy and he started putting the moves on the wrong twin, they never got mad at each other. They always blamed the guy and got their revenge on him.

The twins rarely got upset if one of them didn't like their boyfriends, except in the case of Valentine.

Ripley swooped in and was totally supportive when he sent her that book. She never once said *I told you so.* I would imagine Ripley was unloading everything she didn't say about Valentine for the first time now that he was coming back. Ravyn wasn't going to react well. Valentine nearly drove a wedge between them for the first time. I'd be damned if he did it again.

Felix and I ran out, and the twins were just sitting with everyone laughing. Bram was about to pierce Ripley's nose. Ravyn was relaxed and egging her on. So what the fuck was actually happening right now? I agreed with everything Felix said to me, but I still didn't appreciate being pulled aside and ambushed with it.

Ravyn wouldn't have either. If Ravyn and I happened, it would be on her time. Ravyn loved her romance novels. We'd be a slow burn romance, not a fast burn like Ripley and her familiar. They had to get that.

Ripley's nose was pierced instantly, and she had a lovely blue jewel in her nose. Balthazar was already sporting two spikes in his lips. Reyson was next. I honestly didn't want to be in the same building as the God of Chaos if he had a god tantrum because it hurt. But, oddly, no one else seemed worried Reyson was going to smite the entire room when he got a hollow needle shoved through his nipple.

Reyson seemed to find the clamp amusing. When Bram shoved the needle through, I held my breath, but Reyson started laughing like a madman.

"That was a little kinky. Do the other one now."

Reyson was just so fucking *weird.* And I decided I was going to get my septum pierced.

CHAPTER 6

Ravyn

The piercing party was just my twin sister trying to have a fun way to invite me over and make sure I wasn't going to go back for seconds when Valentine came back. I wasn't even mad about it. If I had listened to her the first time, it wouldn't have blindsided me when he sent me his memoirs about screwing his way through a village of skinwalkers on a dig.

Skinwalkers were highly secretive. They'd been around for ages, and no one knew what they were capable of. They generally lived and married among each other and kept to themselves. If Valentine had been accepted into one of their remote, isolated villages, writing about their culture would have been fascinating.

Instead, he wrote about what skinwalker women were like in bed and how he bravely fought off any men whose women he took to bed. How did I fall for that the first time?

My sister and I got each other. She asked me point blank what my intentions were when Valentine's ship got here. I told her I wasn't sure yet, but it would involve a little revenge and definitely no fucking. That was enough, and we all went and got pierced.

I was so obsessed with Killian's new look. He *rocked* that septum piercing. We were back to our stalemate and at work at the museum. We were cloistered in our archives with my laptop and the one I gave him trying to figure out this mysterious warlock Valentine was working with.

Valentine liked to talk about himself. Honestly, his work was fascinating, and that's my excuse for falling for his crap. I knew about the team he worked with. He was a cheating asshole, but he was thorough. Every supernatural race was represented in case rites needed to be performed and to make sure digs were done with respect to that culture. Every single one of them was an expert in something.

He vetted everyone rigorously. If I looked up any member of his team, there would be peer-reviewed papers in the subject of their expertise. Some of them were published authors, and my sister had their books in her library. Valentine's books were pulp and had a certain reader base. His team wrote much better books.

The Valentine I met a few years ago wouldn't have hired a warlock claiming to be an expert on the Cult of the Aether sisters without receipts to back up that claim. He wouldn't have brought someone on his team that wouldn't even tell him his first name.

I hadn't even met Doctor Key, but I was giving him so much stink eye.

Killian and I were going deep researching this guy. Minerva Krauss first introduced me to the supernatural dark web at the academy when I started my independent study with her on breaking curses. Of course, she made me do a blood oath never to *use* any of the shit people posted there, but it was great for research.

Minerva had to be up to date on all the hexes and curses

people were coming up with because she had a reputation for being the best curse breaker in the world. So instead of waiting for someone to call her, she scoured the dark web to see what kind of nasties people were coming up with to be ahead of the game.

Valentine used it too because people liked to use it to sell dangerous relics. I used it too so that I could find things that needed to be taken off the street and contained in my museum. I was still *super pissed* I'd been trying to find Beatrix Halliwell's missing pendulum for ages, and Dorian Gray was using it on his ceiling fan. That was just blasphemous.

Did Valentine and Doctor Key meet on the dark web? That was the only thing I could think of. Killian and I couldn't find Doctor Key *anywhere*. That probably wasn't even his real name. We couldn't even figure out what he was a doctor of or where he got his doctorate from.

Doctor Key was way sketchier than anything I'd found on the dark web.

"How are we going to figure out his username if we don't even know his first name?" Killian asked.

"First off, he's probably not even a doctor of anything. There are only a few places to do that. Most people go to a magical academy after high school to learn what they need to know because they allow you to specialize. It's usually the healers and scientists that continue their education, but there are programs. There aren't programs for the Cult of the Aether Sisters. They are still the supernatural boogeyman."

"Real doctor or not, he's managed to get on this dig with Valentine and has his ear. Something on that ship shut everything down, and Doctor Key got it running again, so they weren't stranded. He got at least something right because I'm sure the next step after the ship stopped was to sink it."

"It makes little sense. I was around Valentine way more than you were. I *asked* to go on one of his digs. Gertrude probably would have approved it as a work trip because she has a crush on Valentine. He knew damned well I apprenticed with Minerva Krauss and am an expert in my field. He told me his team is a well-oiled machine, and he *never* brings in anyone from the outside unless they've met his team and meshed with them."

"You know what he does on jobs, Ravyn.He could have just said that because screwing his way through villages and getting into brawls with the local men would be hard with you there. But, honestly, it's pretty stupid of him to come back here after he sent you that book. Most sane people leave the state and don't come back if they've pissed off a witch."

I grunted because that was totally true. I could fuck up his whole life with a little bit of his hair and a few ingredients in a mason jar. I still might.

"I didn't get the vibe he was lying about that. Yeah, he's a cheating goat scrotum, but he takes his job seriously."

"Ravyn, he's fucking locals and fighting men on his digs. I'm shocked he hasn't been run out of town before."

"Yeah, me too. I'm not finding anything on the dark web that would make me think Valentine met Doctor Key there. It's five. Ready to head home?"

He nodded, and we started walking home. I couldn't believe we spent an entire day on the dark web and found nothing about Doctor Key. We'd found literally nothing on him so far. Who was he?

Killian and I made a quick dinner and chatted while we ate. I was tired of dancing around things. I *liked* him, and I was tired of pretending otherwise. I didn't want to rush into anything and ruin it. I was perfectly capable of taking things slow. Before he disappeared to his bedroom, I caught his hand.

"Will you sleep in my room tonight? Just to sleep."

He broke into this huge grin and squeezed my hand.

"Yeah, I'd like that."

He'd seen me change clothes before, but I went to my bathroom to change into my pajamas. I didn't own a single set of modest sleeping clothes, but he'd seen those too. When I came back out, he'd stripped down to his boxers.

Killian was reed thin but had wiry muscles. I knew he was strong. I climbed under the covers. He spooned me back and wrapped his arms around me.

"Is this okay?"

It was more than okay. Killian took modern grooming seriously. He had a whole host of manscaping items from the supernatural market, and he smelled amazing. He had me pick out the scent. It was bourbon, sandalwood, tobacco, and vanilla. It also made his hair and skin very soft.

I felt safe like this. Minerva had already called me to tell me she had a weird tarot reading for me. Killian and I had already read the cards and gotten the same reading. Something big was coming our way, and I had a feeling it had something to do with the Cult of the Aether Sisters and the mysterious Doctor Key.

Lying here in Killian's arms, it felt like we could handle anything.

"This is perfect."

CHAPTER 7

Killian

Things had been moving slowly with Ravyn and me, but I wouldn't have it any other way. She wasn't used to me like this. Fuck, I wasn't used to me like this anymore. We were getting used to it together.

We spent the next few weeks waiting for the ship to get here doing the most marvelous things. Ravyn and I were heavily researching the Cult of the Aether Sisters and Doctor Key. That was something we both enjoyed. We'd gone on little dates and held hands. We snuggled every night when we slept, but we still hadn't kissed yet. I was completely fine with that. Back in my day, if you kissed a woman before you married her, it would utterly ruin her. So I could wait until she was ready.

Ravyn and I were both paying careful attention to the stars and our tarot decks. Something major was coming. A rare, full lunar eclipse that hadn't happened in six hundred and fifty years was scheduled to happen again in a few weeks. So it really didn't bode well for us we found some written, oral history that had been passed down in Norway that the supernatural community used the power of the last total lunar eclipse to wipe out the Cult of the Aether sisters for good.

It meant something, but we didn't know what yet.

Valentine was supposed to be meeting Boris, the museum's warehouse guy, to move his shipment into a safe place until Ravyn and I could get to them and start diffusing anything dangerous. He should have been there now.

Ravyn had never been an early riser like her sister. Before all this, she'd hit her snooze button until the last minute, then drag herself out of bed with just enough time to shower and make a thermos of tea. She never had time to make breakfast, and she'd be complaining she was hungry in two hours. She'd been campaigning for a vending machine for the staff since she got hired, but the board thought modern vending machines in a century's old architectural feat like the museum was tacky. I didn't know about tacky, but I knew for damned sure the ghosts at the museum would have had a field day with it.

I had thumbs now, and I woke up the first time her alarm went off. I guess getting up early was still ingrained in me. I always eased out of bed and ensured she had a proper English breakfast, even if I had to pack it up and bring it with us because she wanted five more minutes of sleep. Minerva Krauss converted her to a tea drinker during their independent study, and I knew exactly how she liked it.

I couldn't hear the shower running, so it was a five more minutes type of morning. I started packing up breakfast for both of us when someone started pounding on the front door. Someone had better be dying. Anyone that knew Ravyn knew better than to knock on the door this early. It was a good way to get murdered. It was best not to even talk to her until she had at least half her thermos of tea in her.

I was still in my boxers, but I walked over and flung open the front door to see who had the sheer audacity to knock this early. I was expecting someone from the Paranormal Investigation Bureau because no one else was that stupid.

"Who the fuck are you?" Valentine growled.

Okay, first of all, he had *no right* to go all possessive growly wolf over Ravyn after what he did to her. He hadn't seen her in years. Valentine sent her that signed book then ghosted her. She tried to call him and demand answers why he felt the need to mail her that book, but he never picked up. Valentine pretended like she didn't exist until he needed her expertise and the museum.

Did he even pay attention to her at all when he was here the first time? I gave them their privacy, even though I couldn't stand him. Her sleeping habits had been the same since she was a teenager. She fell hard for Valentine, but she wasn't about to get up early for him.

"Nope. No way. You're supposed to be at the warehouse right now. You'd better get your ass off the front porch and go there now before I make you."

"You're dual natured. That's fascinating. I'd love to know who made you," a deep velvety voice said.

I peered over Valentine's shoulder to see who he had brought with him. There was no way this person could have known I was a warlock who could turn into a bat. The only person on this planet like me was Felix, and when I was around him, his aura and everything about him just screamed warlock. I sensed nothing different from him when he was standing right next to Gabriel.

"I don't know who the fuck you are, but you both need to be at the warehouse."

"How are you going to stop me, pipsqueak? You aren't her type. As soon as she sees me, it's going to be you that gets kicked out, and you don't have any clothes on."

The man with Valentine, who knew I was dual natured had the aura of a warlock. He was just as tall as Reyson but not quite so built. I could tell he was quite powerful. He radiated with it. And he seemed to find this entire exchange hilarious.

"We should leave, Valentine. I wouldn't underestimate this one because you're bigger than him. You're going to lose."

He wasn't wrong. I could beat Valentine with my fists or my magic. I was trained in fighting styles that weren't really taught anymore. Valentine wouldn't know how to defend himself. He'd go for brute strength, and I'd annihilate him.

I only read a bit of his book over Ravyn's shoulder before I couldn't stand it anymore. According to Valentine, he could pleasure any woman, and he'd never lost a fight. I was pretty sure he got his arse beat plenty of times, and that was the real reason they had never run him out of town.

Valentine didn't like hearing he would lose, especially to some green haired warlock he thought was beneath him. He exploded and took a wild swing at my face. I was so hoping he gave me an excuse because I was the one who was with Ravyn after he sent her that signed book and then ghosted her. I knew she had plans, and they were probably subtle, but he could do with a good face punching, and technically he started it.

I darted underneath his fist and gave him a quick jab to the kidneys. I kicked the back of his knees with my bare foot, and he went down. The insane warlock Valentine had with him was laughing like a madman and cheering *me* on, even though Valentine was the one paying his salary. Valentine was petty enough to fire him for that, and if this warlock had spent *any* time around him, he would know that.

He just didn't appear to give a shit. I kind of liked him.

"What the hell is this?" Ravyn demanded.

She was standing in the doorway with bedroom hair and the sexy lingerie she liked to sleep in. We all just kind of stopped to stare at her for a minute. She was glorious in that little black lace number in all her fury. Even the crazy warlock wasn't talking.

He finally stepped forwards and offered Ripley his hand.

"I'm Doctor Key. It's lovely to meet you finally. I hear you're totally brilliant, and I'm curious about your green haired boyfriend. I told Valentine it was a bad idea to come over here before work and surprise you. Unfortunately, your utterly fascinating beau asked him to leave, and things got heated. So we'll be going back to where we *should* have been— overseeing things at the warehouse. Come on, Valentine. I warned you."

The big sulky wolf limped off with Doctor Key, and Ravyn kissed me before I knew what was happening. This was our first kiss, and I was going to make damned sure it was a good one, even if I wasn't quite sure what I did to deserve it. I probably ruined whatever revenge plans she was working on with that brawl.

She pulled away and buried her face in my neck.

"Thanks. I don't want him in my cottage. Did he hurt you?"

"He didn't get a chance, but his knees are going to hurt, and he might piss blood for a little while. Doctor Key is fucking *weird*. He was rooting me on, and he *ordered* Valentine to leave, and he just did it. He knew I'm dual natured, and I can't tell that Felix is when I'm around him."

Ravyn frowned.

"I can't tell with either of you. You and Felix scream warlock from your auras to the vibes you give off. Who *is* this guy? Valentine doesn't take orders from anyone. Do you remember when I introduced him to sushi and told him he wouldn't like it if he ate the entire portion of wasabi they gave him? He ate the whole thing just to spite me, then tried to pretend like his soul wasn't leaving his body as he swallowed it."

"Oh, my Lilith, I forgot about that. He tried to pretend like it was delicious while his nose was leaking snot all up in his chin. It was beautiful."

"So, who exactly is Doctor Key, and why is Valentine letting him boss him around?"

That was a damned good question. And how did he know the truth about me?

I was super pissed. Valentine felt like he not only had the right to knock on my door this early but to get jealous of Killian and try to *hit* him. How many women did he fuck in that book he sent me? I stopped reading after the first graphically described encounter. It wasn't just that it was him cheating on me. He tried to write his sex scenes from his partner's point of view, and he just didn't understand how vaginas worked, even if I had a good time with him in bed.

Killian and I were carrying our breakfast over to the museum. I pretty much loved the fact that he made breakfast for me every morning. We were throwing out theories for Doctor Key.

For starters, he was gorgeous. He looked like Peter Pan if he had grown up to be a seven-foot-tall warlock. He just had this look like he craved chaos and trouble. Killian said he found the whole altercation and him kicking Valentine's ass hilarious. Valentine had an ego. The Valentine I knew would have fired him on the spot for that, then gone after Killian. He didn't do that. He *listened* and left with him.

Doctor Key radiated a *lot* of power. Like, more than any warlock I'd ever met before. Reyson and Lilith level power, but nothing else was adding up. Reyson and Lilith had blinding golden auras. They also had silver eyes. No one else had that color.

Doctor Key's aura was pure warlock, and his eyes were a sparkling green that matched his flaming red hair. Ripley had said nothing about Reyson being able to shape shift into a known species on Earth. She told me about all the other kinky shit he was into. He was obsessed with shifter dick. He checked that off his bucket list, but he'd probably shape shift into a shifter to check all his bases with the knot if it were actually possible.

I always liked to eliminate all possibilities when unraveling the things that came into my museum. Doctor Key was a mystery, but I knew I could get to the bottom of it.

Valentine was nowhere to be found when I got to my office, and Doctor Key was lounging at my desk.

"I thought it wise to leave Valentine at the warehouse. He seems to have certain ideas about what's going to happen while he's here. The witch made an impression on him the last time he was here, and after that entrance you made, I see why. The green haired dual natured creature is quite fascinating to me, and I think we should protect him from jealous wolves. But, he seemed to be able to handle himself just fine. So, what are you and who made you?"

"Nope. No way. You don't get to ask questions. We've been trying to look into you since Valentine called from the ship and said you were his expert on the cult. You don't exist anywhere for a so-called expert. Not even a blog. We can't even find where you got your doctorate, and no one knows your first name."

"Wow, that was a lot and a little personal considering I don't know your green haired friend's name either."

Killian and I exchanged looks. We were trying to keep his dual nature a secret. Hybrids didn't exist in the supernatural world. Trust Reyson to make two of them over his favorite cookies. Some people out there wouldn't be as fascinated with it as Doctor Key. They'd want to hurt Felix and Killian. I'm sure there were some familiars out there that wanted the same thing. Their witch or warlock might not want to give that gift to them for fear their familiars would leave them. That was Ripley's first thought.

"There's no possible way you could know Killian is dual natured. Everything about him is warlock."

Doctor Key stretched like a cat and yawned like this entire conversation bored him.

"Oh, yes. He's definitely a warlock. Anyone who meets him would know that right away. His secret is safe. I know the look of a man who has flown freely with the moon and stars gazing down at his back."

"You're just bullshitting," I scoffed.

Killian was deathly silent because Doctor Key had not only guessed he was dual natured but that he could fly. So who the fuck *was* this guy? He just shrugged.

"Maybe. His secret is safe with me, and I won't press because you don't know me yet. Valentine wasn't paying attention when I said it because he thought Killian was sniffing around his woman."

"Okay, first off, Ravyn is *not* his woman. They got together the last time he was here. Ravyn thought it was a thing, but he ghosted her when he left for a dig, and the only communication she had from him until now was a signed copy of a book he wrote of all the women he fucked while she was sitting here waiting for him to call."

"Yeah, he was kind of a shit at the dig with the locals. I haven't managed to finish one of his books, but they are lies.

By the time we finished, he was banned from every pub in the village and had gotten his ass kicked a few times."

Who *was* this guy? It sounded like he didn't like Valentine any more than I did.

"Why are you here if you don't like him?"

"I get you have your doubts, but I really am an expert on the Cult of the Aether Sisters, even if you've never heard of me before. I wouldn't have inserted myself in this, but this discovery so close to a rare lunar eclipse is serious."

"Yeah, we found they were wiped out the last time this eclipse happened," I said.

"It was a pretty weird coincidence," Killian said.

"No, it's a prophecy. Why do you think the cult fled to a cabin and didn't really fight back when the Vikings had been doing so much with their ships at the time? They could have sailed away somewhere remote and started over. They were quite powerful. They could have taken out countless people with them. By all reports, they locked themselves inside and *let* themselves get burned alive. Why would they do that?"

"Because it's the MO of literally every cult ever? When outsiders come in to stop you, everyone ends up dead," Killian said.

"Yes, because something is sold to the members that they will ascend to a greater plain. The Cult of the Aether Sister did it because they had a prophesy that they would return when the moon goes totally dark again. At the time, no one really understood eclipses. People know *why* they happen now, but they still acknowledge the magic that happens with the moon and the eclipses. But, unfortunately, that particular eclipse didn't happen again for over six hundred years, and shortly before it did, their secret basement was found? I don't like it."

I didn't either. It sounded like a question for Lilith and Reyson. They couldn't tell me much about the cult, but they knew more about the Aether than anyone else I knew. Killian and Felix knew some because they remembered their time there. Reyson said souls went to the Aether until they were born again in a new body with no memories of their past life. That was until Lilith made her witches and gave some of us familiars.

I didn't know Doctor Key. I had a feeling we could be friends, though. It was weird that he didn't share his information, but he seemed to know more than what we found. Still, I wasn't going to break out the god card just yet. Reyson was pretty proud of that fact, but he probably wanted his privacy too.

And I still had some doubts about Doctor Key because I had some insider information.

"Valentine said you did the rites for the cult. How did you do that when everyone says they are dark witches and Killian and I happen to know for a fact that isn't true?"

"So, do I. They were dual natured like your friend. Honestly, I'm shocked no one has figured that out by now. I've heard Lilith is a cheeky little minx, but she's not giving *anyone* bears for familiars. Can you imagine trying to go out in public with a bear? Where is it going to sit? They don't make bear sized pet doors anywhere when they need to take a bear sized shit because there aren't any bear familiars."

How did I miss that? How had *anyone* missed that? Every supernatural establishment had pet doors for familiars when nature called. They were always big enough for a large dog. I'd seen possums and raccoons as familiars, and mine was a bat, but I'd never seen, nor heard of large dangerous predators as familiars except in the cult's case.

"How is that possible?" Killian said. "Everyone knows hybrids don't happen."

The cat was pretty much out of the bag on that one, but it was why everyone missed the connection and thought they were just dark witches. I would have told Doctor Key he was full of shit, but then my sister accidentally resurrected the God of Chaos, and now I knew two of them.

Doctor Key just smirked at Killian because he had somehow figured out his secret.

"Hybrids don't happen when two supernaturals mix. Everyone knows this. Call it the gods making sure their creations were trademarked exactly as their vision. Gods can create hybrids. It's generally considered bad taste to twist another god's creation, but the cult isn't the first time it's happened before."

"What kind of deranged fuck muppet creates bear witches and doesn't step in when they make a cult and make even the Vikings fear them?" Killian said.

Honestly? It sounded like something Reyson would do to impress my twin. If he thought it would get her down the aisle in white, he'd totally make some bear witches. Ripley said he'd never created any magical species before and seemed to take that very seriously.

I saw how Lilith was with hers. She called them her children, and when they did terrible things like abuse an entire race, she only wanted to kill the worst of them and those that didn't fall in line when she told them how things were going to be. If they made a whole cult, Lilith definitely would have stepped in.

"You have to admit. Bear witches are awesome in theory if they aren't totally insane and form a cult. But they aren't *really* bear witches, anyway. Not like the originals. Half of them were modeled after the two of you but created by a different god with different magic. So, they aren't *really* witches or bear shifters. They are more like mages with the ability to shape shift into bears."

"Yeah, but who would do that?" I asked. "There are plenty of things I can do as a witch that I don't go around doing just because I can. That's how you end up in jail."

"They didn't create the cult on a whim. There was probably a logical explanation, and things went wrong. There was also a reason the god that created them didn't step in when they got dangerous."

"Who was it?" I demanded.

I think Reyson still had plans to do some god ass kicking since he found out one had bullied Lilith and turned Gabriel's family into a supervillain. Maybe he knew this mysterious god and could get him in my museum. I was familiar with some of the cult's curses people still used, but not anything they would have kept in their secret basement.

"That's not what we need to be worrying about right now. The site was full of malevolent spirits when I got there. When I saw there was a discovery of a secret room under the floor and there were bodies found, I tried to get in touch with Valentine. I spoke to some assistant quite a lot before I finally got him. After that, it took a lot of convincing to get him to allow me on his dig.

"Valentine had a *lot* of time to be around the spirits of the cult before I called. I warned him to keep everyone away until I could get there. He kept them away, but his people told me he spent a good bit of time at the ruins alone before and after I told him not to.

"Valentine has an entire crew of people to do rites when needed. They said it's standard on any haunted dig and one of the first things they do before starting. It obviously wouldn't have worked until I got there, but he didn't want me to do it right away when I arrived. The only reason it happened was that his entire crew threatened to quit. Which makes me think he was talking and listening to the ghosts of the cult. Valentine might have ulterior motives for bringing those items here. I've been watching him, but he prefers the company of pretty women."

Oh, fuck no.

"You know I hate him after what he did to me, right?" I asked.

"I don't think anyone in this room likes him. We're going to like him a lot less if he uses this museum to bring the Cult of the Aether Sisters back."

Fuck my life.

All the fucked up tarot readings I'd been getting were making sense. I would scream to the stars that The Lovers card that kept showing up had *nothing* to do with Valentine. Ripley and Gabriel both drew that card before they met, and now my twin had an ample supply of dicks around her library.

I would swear on any Lilith relic that card was meant for Killian. He kissed even better than I imagined. And Doctor Key was oddly magnetic. He also knew things I didn't, which made him fascinating. Still, I had standards, and I wasn't going there until he coughed up his first name.

I seriously didn't want to babysit Valentine to find out if he caught ghost cooties. He was a grown ass man and supposed to be a professional archaeologist. *Everyone* knew if you could send ghosts back to the Aether, you did. It was just all kinds of fucked up not to put their souls at rest if you could perform the rites, for starters.

You didn't *speak* to them unless you didn't have a choice. Some of the museum ghosts were pretty great and helped out. There was a ghost of a Puritan child that had been allowed in my cottage since before I got hired. I didn't kick them out when I moved in. They were pretty respectful of my space and enjoyed watching cooking shows. I left the TV on for them when I left for work.

Angry spirits from the whack ass cult people still used to threaten children? Do not pass go. Do not collect two hundred dollars. Do not talk to the fucked up ghosts. And certainly, don't visit them alone. I'm sure he'd seen the witches on his staff commune with spirits before, but there was a reason everyone called us and not wolves when they needed to talk to the dead.

Valentine didn't bring me haunted objects. That bitch probably had a poltergeist hitch a ride over with him, and I couldn't keep a whole wolf in the warehouse I had for that. There wasn't even a shower in there. The plumbing was ancient, and the toilet was constantly getting clogged. We tried to put a microwave in there for the staff, but it kept tripping the breaker.

I'd been petitioning for upgrades to the warehouse, which held our dangerous items until I could diffuse them so the staff that worked there every day could be more comfortable, but the board was super old fashioned. They were all about magical protection, which was excellent, but thought they should be happy their cell phones got a signal in there. Never mind the fact that you had to be really careful taking a shit in there, or you'd need the plunger.

It was time. We were done eating, and Doctor Key had told me a good bit of what I needed to know. But, first, I needed to get to the warehouse and face my cheating ex. My cheating, probably haunted ex. How was this my life right now?

I stepped into the warehouse with Killian and Doctor Key. We spread out the items from the dig on various tables and just radiated nastiness. Valentine was pacing and keyed up. He zeroed in on me right away and tried to get me away from Killian.

"Who is the warlock?" he demanded.

Oh, good. Valentine got warlock vibes off Killian, too, and wasn't paying attention when Doctor Key dropped that he knew Killian was dual natured. Also, who the fuck did he think he was? He didn't own me. Even if he hadn't cheated on me and ghosted me, witches weren't really monogamous.

I was betting odds he wouldn't remember my familiar's name. He probably didn't even remember I had one, so I told him the warlock in my cottage was Killian. I was right.

"Who the fuck is Killian?"

"You are here for work, Valentine. You haven't spoken to me in years. You have no right to demand to know who I spend my time with."

He got right up in my personal space. He used to have this magnetism about him, but I was just repulsed right now. Was it the ghosts of the cult or how he treated me? His aura was just nasty now.

"I thought we had something special the last time I was here?"

I glared at Valentine. Was he fucking kidding me right now? He was not hopping on the Ravyn train this time. If Doctor Key were right, I couldn't risk offending him and breaking his contract with the museum. Gertrude wouldn't sue the shit out of him. She'd blame me. I couldn't say what I desperately wanted to say to him, so I just smiled sweetly.

"We had fun, but that was in the past. Why don't you show me what you brought?"

Since the last time I saw him, Valentine had grown out his mutton chops to a lumberjack beard. He looked so confused as he scratched his beard. Did he seriously not get why I was shooting him down?

"Yeah, um, okay. There's one box with a blood lock I can't

open. My witches don't know how either. There's also another weird box that's in pristine condition. It's like it hasn't been underground for hundreds of years and survived the fire."

"Show me."

Ripley and I could wonder twin the blood lock open now that we had Minerva's diaries. First, I ran my fingers along the box while avoiding the lock. Then, I looked to Doctor Key for the answer.

"What can you tell me about this box?"

Valentine grunted. The last time he was here, I asked him these kinds of questions. Great. Now he was jealous of Doctor Key too.

"It's metal. The same material the Vikings made their swords from. They most likely had a blacksmith forge the box, though most boxes at the time were made from wood. Whatever is in here, they wanted it protected at all costs. If you look closely, there are runes carved into it."

I grabbed a rag and some of the solution I used just for that. I started to clean the box meticulously. I could read ancient Norse, but I couldn't speak it. Killian was with me during my language classes, so he could translate it too. Doctor Key was apparently much more fluent in ancient Norse than either of us because he peered over my shoulder and already had it.

"It's a warning about opening the box to anyone who isn't a member of their coven. It says this box contains terrible knowledge, and if the wrong person opens it, things will be dire for them."

Killian and I gaped at Doctor Key. We were both pretty decent at ancient languages, but we couldn't translate them that fast. He looked at it and read it back to us like he was a native speaker. His accent was purely American unless he was faking it. I had so many questions about this man.

"Ravyn can handle it, though, right?" Valentine said. "This is what she does for a living."

"Your witches and warlocks told you no one could open that blood lock," Key pointed out.

I *could* do it. The question was, *should* I? I normally would have said yes, but this situation was just weird, and I didn't like that prophesy or that eclipse coming up. Still, my curiosity got the better of me.

"I can, but I'm going to need my sister."

"How is Ridley?"

Fucker. He didn't even remember my twin's name, and I know she made an impression on him. We got into this huge fight when she went to a coffee and tea shop with us because I needed her help with something and dumped her coffee in his lap. She chewed him a whole new asshole in front of everyone in the shop because she swore she saw him give his number to the barista when I wasn't looking.

I was furious at the time, but she was just looking out for me. He probably gave his number out plenty of times on our dates. He knew how much my twin meant to me, and he couldn't even get her name right?

"Her name is Ripley, you utter wanker," Killian growled. "You couldn't even be arsed to tell the two of them apart the last time you were here."

"I'm sorry, but I don't even know you. You weren't even sniffing around Ravyn when I was here last."

"Enough, children," Key boomed. "Valentine, things were clearly not roses and puppies the last time you came to this museum. The warlock has already kicked your ass once. We need Ravyn's twin to open this box, and I would imagine she's got strong opinions about you too. We've already got some extremely dangerous objects here. We don't need three witches pissed off at you because of your behavior the last time you visited this museum."

Valentine started sulking like a child.

"I did nothing wrong," he muttered.

Killian and I opened our mouths because that was quite a shit thing to say. Key just had this commanding presence. He raised his hand, and neither of us said what we wanted to say.

"Why don't you take a break and go down to one of the local pubs? Then, after you've had a few, you can think long and hard about why everyone here is so mad at you."

Doctor Key was pretty much my new hero. He was perfectly polite while insulting Valentine and booted him out of my museum. Valentine didn't take orders from anyone. He wasn't a pack alpha, but he liked to pretend he was in the most stereotypical ways possible, like the whip he wore on his hip but couldn't even use in the bedroom for a little kink.

Doctor Key had made him his little bitch throughout that dig, and I was a little grateful. The only reason I hadn't hexed him was that these items were important for my museum. Killian was barely holding it in. I needed Ripley in here to help with the blood lock, and if he tried to pretend like he had done nothing wrong in front of her, things would get ugly.

Key turned to face Killian like ordering Valentine around was totally normal.

"Now that he's gone, you witches might want to burn some sage to cleanse this warehouse of his presence and get your twin in here."

Oh, my Lilith. I was *really* starting to like Doctor Key, even if I didn't know his first name. Ripley was at work. She couldn't leave the library for my museum, even though she totally would if she had someone to cover for her.

"I sent her a text. Unfortunately, she can't come during work hours because she works at the Library of the Profane. But, she'll come when she gets off."

Doctor Key quirked an eyebrow at me.

"You're willing to open a mysterious box from the Cult of

the Aether Sisters after dark? That wolf must be insanely stupid to have ruined things the last time he was here because that's the sexist thing I've ever heard."

Okay, yeah, Doctor Key was fascinating and flirting. I was *going* to find out his first name.

I had originally thought Doctor Key was some sort of fraud, but I was starting to think he was one of those eccentric, brilliant people that kept to themselves until they felt the urge to go out and share their knowledge with the rest of the world. But how had he figured out my secret?

Ravyn and Ripley were both excellent with languages. They studied them at the Academy of the Profane and kept learning after they graduated. I was educated in different languages growing up, but not to the extent I was now learning with Ravyn. I don't think *any* of us could have translated the runes on that box as fast as Key did. Some of them were rusted and hard to make out. We would have had to compare them to other runes to determine what they meant. Key did it in an instant.

I wasn't even mad he was clearly flirting with Ravyn. The twins wanted to let their covens happen naturally. Ripley did with the library guiding her, and I could tell she was quite happy. There were plenty of signs in Ravyn's tarot card readings that fate was about to send her potential coven members.

Doctor Key wasn't a terrible choice, even if he refused to tell us his first name, and he was a little strange.

We couldn't do anything with the metal box with the blood lock until Ripley got here. She promised to come after work. The other item Key wanted us to look at was an ornate puzzle box. There wasn't a blood lock on it, but magical puzzles had to be completed to open it. Ravyn loved games like that, and honestly, so did I.

The thing was, this box looked pristine. It didn't look like it survived a fire and had been underground like the box with the blood lock on it. I had a feeling the consequences for failing a puzzle in this game were deadly, and the Cult of the Aether Sisters weren't really witches like us. Yeah, the witching community had figured out how to break some of their curses and hexes, but we hadn't hit the tip of the iceberg with their magic.

"Should we open this box?" I asked.

Ravyn was going to do it, anyway. She was a little crazy like that. Minerva Krauss saw that same drive in her at the academy and took Ravyn under her wing to harness it safely. At least her thing was diffusing dangerous objects and not stealing cars to drag race because honestly, it could have gone either way.

"Why *wouldn't* we open this box?" Ravyn said, petting it fondly like it was a cat.

We did this dance every time she got a new shipment in. She had an excellent success rate. Ravyn got this job for a reason. I had full faith in her skills. I also had just as many trust issues as she did. People were terrible. We got plenty of lovely religious relics people created to honor the God who created them and some historical items from the estates of famous people, but we also got plenty of terrible shit people created to hurt people. One of these days, she might get something here that hurt her.

"The puzzle box needs to be opened carefully," Key said.

"Something is inside it. A blood lock would have kept people out. If you've figured out how to pick a blood lock, I'm guessing they also knew it was possible or knew it would be one day. Whatever is in *this* box is more important to them than the other locked box."

If Doctor Key was going to be here flirting with my witch, he was damned sure going to *earn* his keep if he would eventually join our coven. I remembered everything from the last time I was alive and my time in the Aether, but the Cult of the Aether Sisters was before my time.

"You're the expert on the cult, Key. Earn your keep," I said.

"And deny this lovely witch the opportunity to do what she clearly loves? We'll help, of course. It'll be a bonding experience. I'm guessing you *were* here the last time Valentine was. I'm also guessing he never saw your face because you are Ravyn's familiar. It's the only thing that makes sense to me, and it's utterly fascinating. I won't press, and I'll keep your secret, but I'm *dying* for the gossip on that one."

How *the fuck* had he figured that out? No one would have drawn that conclusion, and no one would have figured out my secret. This was my second time walking this Earth as a warlock, and I wouldn't have guessed that about Felix or myself. Everything about Felix was pure warlock. Everything about Doctor Key was warlock, but he seemed to know things he shouldn't like Lilith and Reyson.

"We don't even know your first name," I snapped.

"Why is that such a big deal? Have I not been helpful since I got here?"

I pouted because he really had. And I actually liked the man. He recognized Valentine hurt Ravyn and was pissing her off with his jealousy towards me. Key got rid of him, so neither of us had to deal with him anymore.

I got the feeling if we were going to live through this and

not actually revive an evil cult. We weren't going to pull it off without him.

Even if he was super weird about his name.

CHAPTER 11

Ravyn

Key was pretty amazing. Ripley was going to come over as soon as the library closed. Key pretended to leave to get Valentine back to the hotel and double backed. I spoke for all of us when I said I didn't want Valentine to get back to the hotel, wonder why Key wasn't back, and come back to the museum with my twin sister here. There would be blood. I wasn't maiming him because I didn't want to get fired, but my sister didn't work here and would cut a bitch.

He also returned with food from this sandwich shop all the academy students hit up. Ripley and I loved that place and had been fans since we were students. Key got enough for my sister too, which meant a lot to me. He didn't know her, but he knew she was coming straight here without eating.

"You seem like a turkey and avocado on rye with jasmine tea girl," he said, pulling my favorite sandwich out of the bag.

How the fuck had he guessed my favorite sandwich and that I always drank tea? Ripley and I tried every sandwich at the shop, and that one was my favorite.

"I don't know your twin, but she strikes me as a pastrami girl. I got tuna for Killian."

What the actual fuck? Ripley *always* got pastrami. One of the first things Killian wanted to do after he got his body back was eat at our favorite sandwich shop. There were a ton of options, but he ordered the tuna. We witches had our intuition about people, but we had to ask what they wanted to eat.

I wasn't complaining, and I wasn't going to press him. We were keeping secrets because we hardly knew him. He could have his own. I could tell one day we'd be comfortable enough around each other to share them.

The door opened, and my twin sister strolled inside. I saw her take in Doctor Key. Her gaze raked him from head to toe, and then she gave me her trademarked *you need to get that, girl,* look. First, Ripley hugged me, and then Killian.

"We haven't met yet. I'm Ripley. Where is the asshole cheating wolf?"

"Doctor Key," he said, grazing her knuckles with a kiss. "I got rid of him because it upsets your sister. Even with Ravyn's red hair, a man would have to be blind to confuse the two of you, even though you are clearly identical."

"I like this one. You should keep him."

I handed her the pastrami sandwich and opened mine.

"Doctor Key is this big mystery who managed to guess our favorite sandwiches."

"Then you should definitely keep him. Reyson makes our favorite food all the time. It's a perk. And he got rid of Valentine. I like him already."

So did I, but I didn't know enough about him, and I was already taking things slowly with Killian. Was I *really* ready to jump back into the world of dating? Yeah, I was. Why should I let Valentine continue to ruin my life? Not all men were cheaters like him. Ripley's men went all the way to Hell to rescue her. Killian was amazing. Doctor Key was a little eccentric but totally brilliant.

My dating ban was officially over. Valentine could suck it. I was back, bitches.

I leaned over where only Ripley could hear.

"Killian is an amazing kisser. He beat the shit out of Valentine earlier, and it was just so sexy," I whispered.

She held out her fist under the table so I could bump it.

"I fully approve of kissing your familiar and kicking Valentine's ass."

"What made you choose this sandwich shop?" Killian asked.

"Oh, when I went to fetch Valentine from the pub, he had a rapt audience of college girls listening to his woes about how Ravyn didn't wait for him while he was gone. He was drunker than Cooter Brown, and I made him leave. I was almost certain the academy girls would attack me, but I smoothed it over. I asked if they knew the best place to eat, and they told me about this lovely sandwich place. It's quite good."

"What did you get?" I asked.

"Well, I decided to try the turkey and avocado."

My favorite. Ripley pinched me, and I nearly dropped my sandwich. I was used to our pinches and nudges.

"How do you like it?" Ripley said, pretending like nothing was wrong.

"It's quite good. I can see why Ravyn is a fan. I've heard rumors about a speakeasy in the Academy of the Profane. I'm not quite sure what those co-eds were doing at the dirty pub Valentine was at."

"It's in the basement of one of the dorms," I said. "I have fond memories of that speakeasy, but it's not hard to get banned from it. If they thought Valentine was a good idea, they probably aren't allowed."

"Or they are at the age where they think older men are

more exciting, even if they happen to be a big stinking trash fire," Ripley said.

I held up my cup of tea.

"Remember when we were that age?"

She touched her cup with mine and laughed. We were that stupid once.

"Where's Felix and the guys?" Killian asked.

I kicked Killian under the table. I had warned Ripley over text that Key has some weird sixth sense and had guessed Killian's secret. She would have made them stay home, so Felix and Reyson didn't get exposed. I didn't think Key was an enemy, but I didn't know him well enough yet.

"They don't come with me everywhere. I wanted to see my twin, and they are getting ready for the dodgeball game."

I had already bought snacks for that, and Killian and I planned to watch when I got off from work. I threw my garbage in the trash and brushed my hands off. As much as I wanted to hang out with my sister, we needed to get to work. I preferred hanging out at my place or hers.

"Ready?"

"Always."

CHAPTER 12

Key

Witches were utterly fascinating—especially twins. I'd heard rumors about the two that ran the museum and the library here. There were rumblings in the dark web from Dorian Gray and a witch that one of them was vital to toppling deals made with demons. I knew Ravyn's sister had a god at her museum and that they were most likely responsible for her familiar having their body back.

I wasn't going to press and reveal I knew that because I didn't want to be connected to Dorian Gray and that nonsense in the news recently. But, honestly, who did that? You had to be a special kind of stupid to manipulate any kind of God like that.

I knew Ravyn and Killian had been in Hell recently because it had been on the news. Valentine should have known it too, but he acted like neither of the twins hadn't gone through something traumatic. It was not the time for mending romances. She seemed not to be able to stand him, and based on the little I knew, she had every right to.

63

Blood locks had been around for ages. As far as I knew, there was no way of getting into one without the blood of the witch who enchanted it or the people they allowed access to. However, Ravyn seemed confident she could get into this one with her twin.

"Are you sure this isn't going to hurt you?" I asked.

We *needed* to get into that box. The Cult of the Aether Sisters absolutely couldn't be allowed back on the mortal coil, but I wasn't going to risk either twin to do it.

"Are you sure this is wise?" I asked.

The green haired creature just smirked at me. I was almost one hundred percent certain he was a familiar, which was just fascinating. They were way too close to be anything else, and their relationship was more than a little taboo. I loved it.

"Watch and learn."

The twins each cut their palms with an ornate athame. Then, they joined hands and squeezed their bloody fists over the lock. The more blood that hit the lock, the more it started smoking until there was a pop and the lock swung open.

"Ha!" I yelled, shrieking in glee.

How amazing was this woman? Anything could have been in this box. Both twins offered to be here after hours when all the museum staff had gone home to open this lock. They were either utterly insane or completely confident in their abilities to handle whatever was inside.

"Wonder twin magic can fight anything," Ravyn said, holding up her fist.

Ripley bumped it and grinned.

"What's inside the damned thing?"

I snatched the box off the table. Ravyn was already bleeding. If something in this box were going to fight back, it would fight me, not her. I ripped the top off and peered inside.

"It's a book?" I said, pulling it out.

Ravyn peered over my shoulder. Holy shit, she smelled amazing.

"That's not just any book. That's the Cult of the Aether Sister's grimoire," she said. "I know they aren't *really* witches, but they do a lot of things like us."

"Do you know how many bad people are going to want to get their hands on that?" Killian said.

Ravyn tossed her hair over her shoulder.

"People have tried to break into this museum before since they have built it. No one has ever left with anything. Give me that. I need to put it somewhere it can't be damaged to scan the contents. We can start translating it once we have digital copies that are safe to touch. You seem oddly fluent in Old Norse. Can you help with that? Killian and I can translate, but not nearly as fast as you seem to be able to," Ravyn said.

I could do that, but did I want to? Old Norse was as easy for me as breathing. Sometimes, my thoughts were in that language. Whatever spells the cult wrote down in this grimoire didn't need to get out in the world.

Then again, I *needed* that puzzle box opened because I knew what was inside. Ravyn was brilliant, and I was sure Killian was too. I knew neither of them would have any problem translating the grimoire.

The puzzle box needed to be opened *before* the eclipse, but we couldn't play our hand just yet. I needed to translate their filthy spells to figure out how to fight them.

"If someone is going to be scanning this, make sure it's someone you trust. I can translate with no problem. I'm sure you can vouch for every single one of your employees, but I'm telling all of you we need to keep this a secret from Valentine. He lost the trust of his crew on this dig when he kept sneaking off to clearly haunted ruins alone after being told not to, then not wanting to do the rites. I've tried to get him to open up about what he was doing there, but it makes him very crabby pants."

"Oh, good. He's not just a cheater. He's shady too," Ripley growled.

"If Key did the rites, it would have killed any spirit that attached itself to him," Killian said.

"The cult wasn't always dangerous," I said. "They were isolated and kept to themselves for a little while. There were markers in their yard for cult members who died and were buried out there. Plenty of souls were trapped in those ruins because they weren't given the rites, but some of them moved on to the Aether and have possibly been reborn. They wouldn't remember their past, but I think they are vital to the cult's prophecy about returning. I have questions about why the spirits only chatted with Valentine instead of attacking him."

"Maybe you should have led with that instead of acting like you got rid of him because everyone here hates him," Ravyn said.

She looked like I hurt her feeling, and I never wanted to do that. I could tell she was a brilliant witch, and I never wanted her to look at me the way she looked at him. I craved chaos, but I was still a man of honor.

"I *did* get rid of him because he upset you. Seriously, I can't stand Valentine, but I've been attached to him at the hip, trying to figure out why those ghosts didn't attack him when they did to everyone who went by those ruins. They still had more to say because the spirits didn't want to go quietly when his crew threatened to walk if he didn't allow me to do the rites.

"I don't particularly have any desire to babysit a horny wolf who constantly gets into bar fights, but we *need* to find out what the cult wanted with him. Of course, here at the museum, there are fewer distractions for him and gives me more of an opportunity to wear him down, but I see what his presence is doing to you and Killian."

Ravyn gave me this soft smile that melted my heart a little. It was an insignificant gesture, and I did it to be kind, but it seemed to mean a lot to her. I saw her twin sister pinch her where she thought I couldn't see. Ravyn and Killian were clearly together, but Ripley wanted me to join them? How curious. And not totally unwanted.

"I agree we should keep the grimoire a secret from him," Ravyn said. "I appreciate you keeping him away from us after what he did to me, but if you're going to play for our team, you can't keep secrets. You know more about the cult than we do, and you were on that dig. It means a lot to me that you got rid of him, and it's honestly hilarious watching you make him your little bitch, but we all need to find out what the spirits said to him. Honestly, I might be our best shot at that."

"You! Thing One and Thing Two," Ripley said, pointing at Killian and me. "I like both of you, but you'd better have my sister's back while she does this. I know Killian will, but I still have stranger danger vibes with the doctor because we just met."

Did this witch just compare me to a destructive children's book character? She really had no idea how close to the truth she was with that. Still, I'd protect Ravyn even if I weren't fond of her already. I puffed up my chest. I'd impressed Ravyn, but she came as a set. I needed to impress her twin too.

"Killian is not the only one who is capable of giving Valentine an ass beating. Honestly, I'd love for him to give me a reason, and defending your sister's honor is a perfect excuse."

Ripley actually punched me in the arm. Pretty hard.

"I approve. You have my permission to sniff around my twin and find out if she digs you for her coven."

Well...thanks? Getting invited to a witch's coven had never happened to me before, but I was pretty sure it never involved assault from a sister. I liked the twins. They were direct, powerful, and brilliant. Ravyn was quite lovely.

And any witch who knew the language of the Norse Gods well enough to use it at work was speaking directly to my soul.

My twin was nothing but persistent. When we both had shit luck with men, she was fine with my dating ban. But, now that she had five hot men worshipping her, she wanted the same for me. I was always her wingman when she went trolling for dick at bars. A girl needed backup to weed out the weirdos, and *plenty* of weirdos were interested in both of us.

Once, while I was running interference for my twin, a vampire wearing a pink top hat tried to get me to go home with him and do all kinds of fucked up things with silly string. I wasn't about to kink shame someone for their silly string proclivities in the bedroom, but I didn't really want to take part in it.

If I ended up with what my sister had men wise, it would be on my terms. Doctor Key was beautiful, fascinating, and brilliant, but he wasn't totally honest with us. I understood he didn't voice his suspicions about Valentine in as much detail as he did tonight because he tried to make my museum a safe space by removing Valentine.

I was a big girl. I could deal with that wolf turd if he went from serial cheater to manipulated by the ghosts of a dangerous cult. Still, it meant a fucking lot that Key was willing to risk it because he knew something bad went down between us.

The grimoire was safely contained where the elements couldn't hurt it. We had this really great vampire named Sasha on staff who was a master at making digital copies of anything that came in on parchment without damaging it. She liked to read the grimoires and look at the illustrations for historical purposes, but she had no interest in releasing the contents of them to the general public. So I trusted her implicitly with this grimoire.

We were about to wrap up and go home to watch the dodgeball match. My favorite teams weren't playing, but maybe someone would surprise me and end up at the playoffs.

I didn't quite want to call it a wrap just yet. Who *was* Doctor Key? How did he manage to guess everyone's favorite sandwich? I wanted to know more.

"Want to come watch the dodgeball game with us?" I asked.

"England isn't playing, but it should still be a good match," Killian said.

"Yes, but Norway is, and that's my team. I'd love to."

He rooted for Norway and was fluent in Old Norse? I wanted to know more. Everyone had a favorite dodgeball team. Ripley and I both rooted for England because our familiars were born there. We were decent players in high school, but the Academy of the Profane didn't have a team because they prided themselves on academics.

I'd never met a single person who rooted for Norway's dodgeball team before. I watched when they played because dodgeball matches were always exciting, but they'd never done anything on the field to convert me.

"Should I stop for snacks?" Key asked.

"Nah. I'm fully prepared for that. Ripley and I take our dodgeball matches seriously. We always watch together when England is playing. She's watching with her harem tonight."

"I do watch the news, Ravyn. She seems to have recovered from her ordeal just fine. How are you holding up?"

Shit. Kaine did those press conferences after my sister got kidnapped. I didn't think it would make international news, but Key heard about it, anyway. He knew full well my sister was shacking up with a god. I still didn't know how he figured out Killian was dual natured, but he knew *how*.

And he hadn't demanded to meet Reyson. He didn't ask Ripley a single question about him. When he dropped the little tidbit that he knew my sister was dating a god, he asked how *I* was doing after going to Hell to rescue my sister.

"The men that took her are epically dead now. It sparked an entire revolution in Hell and freed the Hellhounds. We got to meet Lilith, and she's pretty damned cool."

"Fate is a strange beast. I can't imagine the thought process of people that think kidnapping someone's loved ones and that they think it will end well for them. You have to be a special kind of stupid to do that when a god is involved. Unfortunately, some of the gods are terribly petty and have no problem hurting their own family."

"I heard about that with Lilith."

"Not Lilith. Look deeper into the Norse gods. They did some pretty terrible things to each other."

"Where are you from, Key?" I said, unlocking my front door. "You seem to know a lot about ancient Norse culture."

"Just paying homage to my roots."

A half answer.

"Why haven't you published everything you know?" Killian asked from the kitchen as he started bringing the snacks out.

Key just shrugged.

"I share what I know when it's needed. I don't feel the need to write books or get quoted in other people's work. It just feels arrogant. I also have a law license. Sometimes, I like to do that. It's fun toppling insurance companies or ruining a rapist's day."

Key didn't look that much older than I was. How had he found the time to cram that much knowledge in his head? I was constantly learning and spent my whole life studying, but sometimes, a bitch needed Wikipedia.

"Have you tried toppling the patriarchy?" I asked.

"I did get a judge who had a history of giving rapists probation kicked off the bench."

I held up my fist for a bump because I was so here for that. Killian plopped next to me on the couch and threw his arm around my shoulder.

"Norway is your team?" he asked.

"I *know* they haven't been to the playoffs in ages, but someone just needs to remind them that there was a reason the Vikings were once feared. Supernaturals took up that vocation too. The new forward on Norway's team is one to watch. She's starting tonight. She's a lovely siren. Mark my words. You need to watch that one."

The game was starting. There were five balls in dodgeball. The golden ball was what you scored with. The other four balls had various magical properties. Players would grab the ball and throw them at players to stop them from scoring. You could use any of your magical gifts in this game because it was *supernatural* dodgeball. We existed way before humans started throwing rubber balls at kids' heads, like Beyla explained to us.

The team gathered on either side of the field in their positions. The balls shot out of the ground, and everyone scrambled to catch one. Key was right about Norway's siren. She was spectacular. Killian and I were keyed up and screaming at the television.

When the match was over, Norway had won by a huge lead. I grabbed Killian and kissed him and then threw my arms around Key. Then, I realized what I was doing. Shit. Were we at the huggy part of our relationship? I literally just met him. I cleared my throat and pulled away.

He smiled at me when I tried to die in my couch cushions. Maybe it wasn't a bad thing. He tucked my hair behind my ear.

"I like hugs."

This big, massive mischievous man liked hugs. I was here for that. It was late, and Key excused himself to go home. I looked at Killian and knew what I was going to do tonight.

My sex ban had gone on long enough. Now that I kissed him, the flood gates were open.

CHAPTER 14

Ravyn

I hadn't had sex since Valentine sent me that book a few years ago. Was it like riding a bicycle? Could I still suck dick like a champ? There was only one way to find out. As soon as the front door closed, I climbed into Killian's lap and started kissing him. His hands went to my ass, and he squeezed.

"Are you sure?" he asked.

"Shut up," I growled.

Killian wrapped his arms under my thighs and stood up with me. He was a lot stronger than he looked. He carried me to the bedroom with me kissing his neck. He laid me on my back and started kissing me. The boy could certainly kiss.

I went straight for his zipper, and he grabbed my hand to stop me. Why? I needed to know I could still suck dick, and I wanted his.

"I want to taste you first," he said.

Or we could do that too. I started stroking him through his pants.

"A hot little sixty-nine?"

Killian growled. He snapped his fingers, and we were both

75

naked. I barely looked at him naked when Reyson changed him, but I was certainly looking at him now. He was long with lean muscles. I trailed my fingers down his washboard abs to his cock. That was... big. Killian was packing. It was long, thick, and a little unexpected.

"Holy shit."

"I know," he smirked. "Before we go there, you'd better do your birth control spell."

"I did it on the couch while you and Key were watching the game. I had plans."

It just involved holding a certain crystal that I had plenty of and whispering your intention to the stars. I had one on the table behind the couch.

"You sneaky bitch. I love it. I didn't notice. Do you think Key did?"

I started nibbling on his ear.

"Is it bad that I found the whole thing kinky, and I hope he did?"

"He's not a terrible choice if he ever decides to tell us his first name. I approve just as much as Ripley does."

"Baby steps. I've only just decided I'm no longer letting Valentine ruin my love life. I hadn't had a good orgy since that full moon party before Valentine got here, but I just want it to be you and me for now. At least until he coughs up his first name."

Killian was doing the most *amazing* things to my nipples. I groaned and arched my back. I didn't regret my nipple piercings in the slightest.

"Why do you think he won't tell us his name?"

"Killian! We are both naked, and you know the last time I had sex. I *do not* want to talk conspiracy theories over his name."

"Me either, but I *know* the last time you had sex. I haven't had it since the last time I was alive. What if we both die from it?"

Oh, shit. I hadn't even thought about that. It had only been a few years for me, but it had been centuries for Killian. What if I'd forgotten everything I learned at the academy when it came to men and was totally shit at this? He saw me chewing my bottom lip. He knew that meant I was worrying about something. Killian knew me well enough to know what I was thinking too.

Killian wrapped his arms around me and rolled us so I was on top of him. He started tickling me, and he knew damned well I was ticklish.

"We're both nervous and thinking we're going to botch this. We probably won't. I'm sure I was shite my first time because they didn't exactly teach young men how to pleasure women back then, but I learned. I *remember*. So do you. It's going to be fabulous. Now sit on my face."

I guess it was just like getting back on the horse. Or, in this case, a warlock's face. I'd done this before. I was glad I was breaking my dick fast with Killian. Aside from my twin sister, there was no other person on this planet I was closer to.

I needed to thank Reyson for this. What the shit did you get a god for making it possible to fuck your familiar? Gift cards were impersonal, and it's not like he needed money when he could conjure what he wanted out of thin air. A gift basket full of really weird junk food from around the world that he hadn't thought to try yet? Sold.

I straddled Killian's face and draped myself across his stomach so I could get to his cock. Killian was quite blessed in the cock department. Would it be weird to text Lilith and thank her for that? Ooh! He was also *quite* talented with his tongue.

Killian would be a challenge as far as back on the horse blow jobs went, but I was feeling ambitious tonight. I wrapped my hand around his cock and took it in my mouth. Killian let out a little growl and sucked my clit between his teeth. I shuddered and squeezed his balls.

I wasn't sure why I was so worried about this. Maybe because it was Killian, and this wasn't some random bar hookup. This was important. Killian meant more to me than Valentine ever did, and I knew for sure he felt the same and wouldn't step out.

There was this synchronicity between us. There always had been, but it was extreme when we were like this. Where our skin was touching felt like it was electric. Killian felt it, too, because he was ravenously licking my clit and thrusting into my mouth. It was intense, and it felt amazing.

Killian was frenzied, and I wasn't going to last much longer. I didn't think he was either. I felt him twitch in my mouth, and shortly before he exploded, he bit down on my clit, and I did too. Oh, holy fuck. My celibacy had been worth it just to get to this moment.

I crawled off his face with my whole body shaking and snuggled into his chest.

"Oh, my Lilith, you definitely haven't forgotten a single thing," I said.

"Neither have you. That was superb."

"Maybe Valentine happened because I was supposed to wait for you."

"No. Never say that. I wouldn't have been the slightest bit upset if you already had what Ripley has when this happened, and you let me join. You're a witch, Ravyn. You're not meant to be alone. I got why you did it, but I hated watching it."

"Yeah, well, that's over now."

"I'm glad I got to be a part of you ending your dick exile."

"Good. I'm totally wrecked right now, but there are so many things I want to do with that monster."

"And we will. Go to bed, Ravyn. It's late, and we're going

to have to figure out how to manage Valentine tomorrow if Key isn't sending him away."

There were so many things I'd *like* to do with that cheating wolf but babysitting him because he was dumb enough to listen to deranged ghosts was not on my top ten.

CHAPTER 15

Killian

I was feeling all kinds of blessed when I woke up. I left a little offering on our altar to Lilith. Maybe I should text her a little thanks. Should I contact Reyson instead? He was the one that randomly started giving familiars their bodies back.

Ravyn and I had our morning routine down, and thankfully, there were no stupid wolves banging on the door this time. I had already packed breakfast up by the time she was out of the shower, and we started walking to the warehouse.

Key and Valentine were already there. They didn't have keys, but they apparently didn't feel the need to knock so someone could let them inside. Ravyn scanned her security card on the lock and let us in.

She had already moved the grimoire somewhere it would be safe and texted Sasha it was there to start scanning. Ravyn asked her to keep it on the down-low for now. We still needed to find out what was going on inside Valentine's head before we told him about the grimoire. He couldn't use the spells in there, but there were plenty of wicked witches out there who would love to get their hands on it.

I set our breakfast down and started pulling trays out. Valentine grunted and bumped my shoulder. This aggro fucker was about to get laid out on the floor.

"I brought donuts and coffee," he grunted, setting his boxes down.

Did he pay attention to her at all the last time he was here? Ravyn didn't eat a lot of sweets, and she always drank tea. On the rare occasion she ate something with sugar, she'd always crash and get sleepy a few hours later. She knew this and rarely did it except for holidays. Ravyn had seen a healer about it. She was totally healthy, but sweets didn't really agree with her.

It had been like this for ages, even when Valentine was here last time. I was fairly certain she had told him about it too. Key was nothing if not perceptive. He had no way of knowing why I was giving Valentine the stink eye, but he knew something was wrong.

Key opened the box of donuts and pulled one out.

"Ooh, a maple bar," he said, disappearing with his donut, and I'm pretty sure a coffee Valentine meant for Ravyn.

There were only enough donuts in the box for two people, and he only got coffee for him and Ravyn. Valentine scowled at Key, but he didn't fight him. Instead, he just stood there sulking until he noticed the box from last night was open.

"You got it open? What was inside?"

I didn't like the look that was in his eyes as he stared at the open box. We already came up with a plan for this before we left last night. Ravyn smiled sweetly at him, and I just wanted to vomit. I knew she was playing him, but I wanted *my* Ravyn back, who was plotting her revenge.

"Let's eat breakfast first, huh? Didn't you always used to say that you couldn't function without a nutritious breakfast?"

Valentine's eyes never left the metal box. Yeah, this shady

motherfucker was definitely up to something, but he also knew he wasn't getting his candy without Ravyn. He'd signed a contract with the museum, and these items were now ours. He could have left now, but he needed a lot of the information Ravyn would give him for quotes when he did press conferences. She was a whole hell of a lot smarter than Valentine was.

She touched his arm. I *hated* that. I didn't have a problem with her touching other men. It was him I didn't like.

"Didn't you say it affects your wolf if you don't eat in the morning?"

He turned and plastered this totally fake grin on his face. I didn't trust him at all.

"You're right. Doctor Key took your coffee. And my maple bar."

Remind me to get Key a gift basket later. I slid her breakfast over and sat next to her on the table. Key had disappeared with Valentine's maple bar to poke around with the relics. I wasn't worried about him alone with this stuff.

"That's okay. Tell me about you. What have you been up to since you've been gone? What made you decide to go to Norway?"

I saw Key start inching his way closer. Valentine was ignoring both of us. He had what he wanted. The rapt attention of a beautiful woman, even if she was faking it. Ravyn was the only one who could get this information out of him, as much as I hated to admit it.

"So, I did one of those ancestry tests. Did you know my relatives came from that area? They were probably fierce Vikings. I went on vacation and started scouting around for places to possibly do a dig. I checked out the village where the Cult of the Aether Sisters lived. Most people don't live there anymore because of the ghosts.

"I'm a wolf. I'm not scared of a few ghosts. So I went to

check out the ruins. The ghosts were there, but they didn't attack me. They told me where to dig, and I found the room underneath the floor. I called my team out, and the rest is history."

Ravyn delicately bit into a piece of bacon and pretended to be super impressed by that. Key and I weren't saying a damned thing, even though we had questions. This was something only Ravyn could do.

"Why do you think the spirits talked to you instead of attacking you?"

"Because they recognized an alpha, of course. It's the only thing that explains it."

I tried not to choke on my eggs. Valentine wasn't born an alpha. Nor had he challenged one for their position. He wasn't remotely an alpha. Ripley dug into him after he destroyed Ravyn's heart, and he was exiled from his pack because they didn't want him anymore. Probably because he couldn't keep his dick in his pants and liked to start fights.

He liked to pretend that was just what shifters did, but it wasn't even remotely true. Most of the shifters I'd met would have found that offensive. Bram had been nothing but great to Ripley, even if he was a Hellhound and not a wolf.

Key caught my eye, and we shared this disgusted look. He knew damned well Valentine wasn't an alpha too. Valentine had adopted every negative stereotype people who were racist against shifters liked to say and acted like he was proud of it. Ravyn was super into the werewolf porn at the Library of the Profane, and I'd read some of it over her shoulder. Those books got some things about wolves completely wrong for erotic purposes but still preserved werewolf culture.

Honestly, I'd never understood Valentine or why he perpetuated that nonsense with pride.

"You've always been my favorite alpha," Ravyn purred.

"The Cult of the Aether Sisters has always fascinated me. I can't believe they spoke to you instead of attacking you. I'm pretty sure other people have been to those ruins and didn't find out about the basement. That's utterly brilliant. Did they spill any secrets no one else knows?"

I loved watching Ravyn at work. She was brilliant at the museum, but both of the twins had weaponized their sexuality if a man was up to no good. I *hated* watching her pretend to be into Valentine after what he did, but he was eating it up. If anyone was going to be left with their dick in their hands and a broken heart when this was over, it was going to be him. So, I dealt with it. Key didn't look like he enjoyed this any more than I did.

"I haven't been able to find it, but they told me that their grimoire was in the ruins and that I needed to locate it. I'm guessing it's in that weird puzzle box that looks like it hasn't aged a day. Of course, they wouldn't have put it in a box without magical protection. I'm not sure how you opened a blood lock, but I *know* you'd tell me if you found something as important as their grimoire."

Yeah, you know nothing, Jon Snow. Key ratted your ass out. I didn't know what shit show was in that puzzle box, but it was probably way worse than their grimoire. Valentine was right about one thing. They put their grimoire in a metal box that managed to be airtight despite the time they made it.

The grimoire was still in fairly decent condition for Sasha to scan. Unfortunately, it wasn't given the same consideration as whatever they put inside the puzzle box. The puzzle box had so much magic in it, there wasn't a speck of rust on it like the box with the grimoire.

"I agree. The discovery of their grimoire would be a major find. But, even if you're an alpha, you still aren't a witch. So why would they want you to have their grimoire?"

I didn't like what Valentine's aura was doing. I'd never really liked it, even before he broke Ravyn's heart. It was starting to twinge black. I'd seen that before, and it was never good. His aura wasn't bad before, or Ravyn would never have fallen for him. I just hated everything about him, including his aura, because I thought he was wrong for her, and I was right. His aura was having things creep into it like he was getting into dark shit he shouldn't.

All three of us were witches. He could hide that from plenty of people, but never to us.

Ravyn was playing him brilliantly. I wanted to vomit when she started stroking his arm. I knew *why* she was doing it, but I didn't want her near him.

"I know I'm not a witch and can't use what's in there, but *you* are. You could use what's in that grimoire."

Ah. *There* it was. Valentine didn't choose this museum because he wanted to mend fences with Ravyn after what he did. He wasn't even trying to be nice with breakfast because of their past. He needed the *best* museum and a strong enough witch to cast whatever spell was in that grimoire the cult whispered to him.

I had a feeling it had something to do with the eclipse and the right spell. Coming back from the dead was impossible without necromancy done right. Ripley and Ravyn were both pretty amazing at that. While Ripley had an entire room at her library to help people with that to cut down on revenants, the Museum of the Profane had a strict *No Necromancy* policy with remains that came in.

Valentine had brought an entire case full of bones. No one at the museum was dumb enough to bring them back. Valentine knew necromancy was forbidden at literally any museum he would have brought something to. He might not have paid much attention to Ravyn's likes and dislikes the last time he was here, but he had to know she wouldn't do it.

I had a feeling we were missing a piece, and it had something to do with that puzzle box. I didn't like it.

Of two things, I was certain. One, I really didn't want Ravyn opening that puzzle box. Two, I knew damned well she would do it anyway, no matter what anyone told her.

CHAPTER 16

Key

Most people didn't trust me for excellent reason. I was a duplicitous creature that did things on a whim just for fun, and then things blew up in my face. I lied for fun. When I chose cases to represent as an attorney, it was for the sheer joy of screwing up the legal system.

I was helpful when I wanted to be, but only on my terms. I wasn't at this museum to be helpful. This was personal. I was used to people not trusting me. I could count on one hand the people I knew that *I* trusted, and I knew a lot of people.

I wanted to be honest with the witch and her dual natured friend, but I couldn't be sure I could trust them yet. But, I needed to trust them soon because I was tired of pretending. I knew the connotations that came with my name. They'd know me immediately and all the stories about me that were floating around out there.

I needed them to get to know me first. I wasn't all bad, and I really was here to stop the Cult of the Aether Sisters from returning. I knew them better than anyone alive. If they had delivered a prophecy, they had the tools to know it had a very good chance of coming true. It probably would unless I stepped in.

Ravyn was magnificent. She was a brilliant witch if she could pick a blood lock with the help of her twin sister. I was guessing Old Norse wasn't the only language she knew, but the fact that she did spoke to my soul. She was masterfully manipulating Valentine. He was eating it up and telling us exactly what we needed to know.

You couldn't even tell she probably wanted to dissect his testicles while he was still awake and replace his eyeballs with them. That was actually a good idea. I needed to file that away for later in case someone pissed me off.

I could tell Killian didn't want to open the puzzle box. I had a feeling Ravyn was going to do it, anyway. I *needed* her to open that box, but I didn't want to make an enemy of Killian. I liked him. I could see us being friends. If things worked out, he might end up on my one hand of people I trusted.

Valentine needed a witch to pull this off. He made it seem like he was desperate to rekindle things with the one that got away this entire trip. He was miserable about waxing poetic about all the good things about her that he clearly just made up because now that I met her, most of it was wrong.

That stupid motherfucker had tried to manipulate me, and I didn't like it. It was pretty clear that he paid little attention to what she did and didn't like the last time he was here. I'd picked up more about her in the short time I'd been here than he seemed to know.

I had to stop him from knocking on her door again with his donuts. Valentine must be totally clueless. We all saw her burst outside in her sexy pajamas when she heard the fight. The witch enjoyed her snooze button. Killian clearly got up early and made her breakfast so that she could sleep late and get to the museum. Any idiot with half a brain could tell that.

I pulled Killian aside while Ravyn was working Valentine.

"Whatever we do, we cannot let Valentine get his hands on that grimoire."

"I know. I have a feeling he wants her to do necromancy, but it's against the rules here. She wouldn't unless she was forced."

My gaze strayed to Ravyn.

"Something tells me you can't force that witch to do anything she doesn't want to."

"No. She's nothing but stubborn."

"I'm also pretty sure she can protect herself just fine, but we can have her back."

"Mm. I don't think she should open that puzzle box."

That was a big no for me. I needed that box open. I was the one who made it, after all.

CHAPTER 17

Ravyn

Valentine had spilled a good bit, but not all that we needed. So I invited Key back to my place after work again for a little subterfuge and plotting. We were going to need him if we were going to stop Valentine and the cult. Honestly, I just liked having him around. It was pretty amazing watching him steal Valentine's bribery donuts and coffee.

I offered to cook dinner for everyone, but Key asked if he could borrow my kitchen and cook for us. I had no problem with that. He ended up an amazing chef. We didn't really talk about work over dinner. Key was more interested in getting to know Killian and me. Oddly, he still wasn't asking about our experience in Hell. I didn't know a single warlock that wouldn't want to know what Lilith was like in person.

"So, do tell," Key said. "Why did you shun the wolf's donuts?"

"Sugar crash. It happens every time. And then I get a zit right here," I said, pointing to my chin. "Ripley and I are identical, but she can eat just as much sugar as she wants with no problem."

"Valhalla, forbid we mar that perfect skin," he said, tipping his wine glass at me.

There was another Viking reference. Who was this guy anyway? I could play the same game he was. He wanted to get to know each other, so we would.

"How do you know so much about the Vikings?"

"Valentine isn't the only one whose roots go back there. You could say my soul was forged there."

Fair enough. Just then, my phone rang, and it was Ripley. I needed to get that. So I picked up right away.

"Hey, I invited Beyla over this weekend for some magic lessons. Remember when Kaine said her parent's human friends were giving him shit with child protective services? We need to teach her how to protect herself. Especially if her crazy ex comes back in the picture."

"Good call. I bought her a witchy care package with the basics when we were getting Killian new glasses."

"Which he looks *adorable* in."

"And out of them."

"Girl, you'd better spill."

"I'm having dinner with Killian and Key."

"Later then. And I approve inviting Key back to your place."

"You've said that multiple times. Right now, we're trying to figure out what Valentine wants with the grimoire. He wants me to do the magic in there, probably to bring them back."

"Good luck with that. I can't even get you to let me borrow those kick ass black fuck me boots you found at the witch market," Ripley said.

"Oh, I'm definitely not going to do it. I just haven't weaseled out of him what his end game is."

"Well, get to work. We're going to do Saturday brunch in the gardens at the library to teach Beyla. Kaine is bringing her.

I figured we could start with the basics of protection. I'm sure Kaine has dragon things at his house doing that, but it could do with a witchy boost to help keep the humans away."

"We'll be there."

"Invite Key but tell the stupid wolf to say at his hotel."

"That might be weird. What about Reyson and Felix?"

"It's not like he hasn't figured a good bit of that out by now. I didn't get bad vibes off him."

"Neither do I. I feel like we can trust him, but he's weird about his name."

"Reyson is weird about his Oreos, but I love him anyway."

"Yeah, but Reyson is older than the universe. He's *allowed* to be eccentric."

"So is Doctor Key, asshole. You know witches can do all kinds of shit with a name. We're probably the weird ones giving it out everywhere. So many shady ass people came into my library after Silvaria corrupted the spirits, and they all know my name. He's allowed to be weird about his name. Key is probably figuring out if he can trust you. He's also a sexy beast. You should let him."

That was an extremely good point that I hadn't thought about. Using someone's true name to utterly destroy them had been forbidden for a long time, but that didn't mean someone wasn't going to do it anyway. Key oozed power. Did someone try to take him out with his name to even the playing field?

"Maybe some other time, but Killian and I will be there."

"Okay, but if he's joining your harem, he's going to have to meet mine."

"Ripley! I'm not even there yet."

"Reyson said it's coming, and you know how he is with his possibilities."

"Tell Reyson to keep his possibilities to himself when it comes to my love life. It's too much pressure."

"Fine, but when a god tells you hot dick is headed your

way, and you already have a fine specimen in your museum, you should jump on that."

"I'm a scorned woman, Ripley. Unfortunately, I had to put my revenge plans on hold because Valentine was dumb enough to get manipulated by ghosts. So let me take this on my own time."

"At least tell me the sex was good."

"I kind of wanted to text Lilith for blessing that boy with skills and a massive cock."

"You totally should, but only if you send me a screenshot of her reply."

"You know I'm your wingman for whatever stupid plot you want to drag me into, but I'm going to pass on texting our creator about my boyfriend's dick."

"I love that you are calling him your boyfriend now."

"I have my own plot to come up with. Valentine isn't just a cheater anymore."

"Want Reyson to kill him? No one will ever find the body."

"Not just yet. I know he hasn't told us everything."

"Well, go get it, girl. And get to know the hot warlock."

"I'd be doing that right now, but I'm hearing out your opinions on my love life because I love you."

"Noted. I'll let you go. You have two hot warlocks in your cottage. Use your time wisely, young Jedi."

I laughed and hung up the phone. I went into my living room. Key and Killian were lounging on my couch, looking like old friends. They were polar opposites.

When Killian first showed up as my familiar, he spoke like someone from centuries ago. But, he quickly picked up on modern slang, and now he spoke like he had been born the same year I was. If it were a good one, he'd break out burns from his time, and I found it hilarious.

Key never outright insulted Valentine to his face like

Killian and I did to each other all the time. It was subtle, but he did it all the time without Valentine noticing. I had a feeling if he ever did, Killian and I were going to need more than a fist bump to congratulate him.

"What have you two been plotting?" I asked.

Key just winked at me like he heard my entire phone conversation, even though I had left the room.

"I imagine it's nothing as salacious as what you and your twin were discussing."

There was no possible way he could have known if my twin sister could have invited herself here, she would have used Reyson to trap us in my cottage and disappeared all my clothes until a threesome happened. I knew she just wanted me to be happy, and as far as threesome fantasies went, that was probably a *really* hot sandwich to be in the middle of.

I was still a little gun shy. I knew Killian wasn't going to step out on me. I had a feeling Key wouldn't either. He seemed to dislike Valentine for doing that to me. I just didn't *know* yet. So, I changed the subject.

"We're doing brunch at the library to teach little Beyla some witchcraft."

"Excellent. You can give her your care package. You know they aren't teaching her magic at high school."

"A high school witch with magic? How did that happen?" Key asked.

Killian and I filled him in on Beyla. How her parents raised her human and her idiot human boyfriend decided to ruin an opportunity for her to dance professionally by breaking both of her feet. Then, her parents got into a fatal car accident, and she took too many pills because she thought her life was already over.

Kaine didn't want that to happen again, and neither did Ripley nor me. So we would weave an entire support system around that girl until she was a badass witch and a professional dancer.

"That's unfortunate," Key said. "Has the dragon who adopted her eaten that boy who broke her feet?"

"He's missing. Kaine said he didn't do it. Kaine is a pretty important officer of the law, but he came with us to Hell," I said. "Kaine pretty much reveled in going rogue with his dragon in Hell. *If* he got revenge on that boy for hurting Beyla, he'd be bragging about it."

"I have a big problem with men who hurt women. That goes for physically and emotionally. I've gone to extremes to prevent arranged marriages the woman didn't want. Someone needs to find this boy and fling him into the sun."

That was pretty fucking romantic. No one really did arranged marriages and dowries anymore except supernaturals with old money whose ancestors were famous. The rest of the civilized world realized you probably shouldn't marry your third cousin because you were worried about poor genes from the common folk.

Their kids were so brainwashed, most of them just went through with it, even if they couldn't stand the person they were supposed to marry. A few hated it and spoke out against it. I could imagine some of the things Key had to do because some of the kids I went to school with at the academy really didn't want to marry their buck-toothed distant relative and were told to do it or be disowned. The supernatural community loved a good shunning.

"I'm dying to hear that story," I said.

"Well, it's quite a long story that involves massive amounts of trickery. You might think less of me once you've heard it."

"Okay, now you have to tell us. It sounds juicy."

"That is a story for another night. The eclipse is coming up, and we need a plan."

"Valentine needs a witch, and I don't intend to comply."

"Eventually, he's going to figure that out. He hoped to use your previous relationship to get you to help him, but he'll realize it's over, and you won't break the rules. *You* might not be a corrupt witch, but it wouldn't be hard for him to find one. How safe is that grimoire?"

"Sasha is trustworthy and capable of fighting off a wolf. She works in an area of the warehouse I haven't taken Valentine to. Her office has its own entrance, and he's never seen her. Even if I hadn't already warned her, she usually stays in her office with her toys."

"That's good, but you managed to get his mind off what was in that box for today, but he's going to ask again. It can only be in two places, and we need to get the puzzle box open before the eclipse."

"I don't think we should open that puzzle box," Killian said.

"Oh, but we absolutely should," Key said.

I was with Key on this one, and Killian knew it. We needed to know what was so important that the Cult of the Aether Sisters hid it in a magical puzzle box.

"Maybe we can lie and say we found something else in the box. I might have something I can swap," I said.

"Leave that to me," Key said. "I'll sneak it in tomorrow."

What was Key doing with ancient Viking relics, and why would he part with them like this? I liked him the more time I spent around him, but I also had a million more questions.

CHAPTER 18

Karyn

Killian had breakfast prepared again when I woke up. He must have been trying to make a point because he made enough for Key, but not Valentine. Man, no one here liked that wolf. He packed it up in his backpack, and we walked over holding hands.

Valentine and Key were waiting. I smiled sweetly and hugged Valentine. I turned my head when he tried to kiss me. Gross. He was a decent kisser, but I knew where that mouth had been. I got through one chapter of that book he sent me before I heaved it across the room and shrieked to the cosmos. Valentine grunted in frustration that he didn't get my mouth.

"Is there any way we could get a key to the warehouse?" he asked.

The last time he was here, he started staying with me at my cottage after a few days. He walked over with me and didn't have to wait for anyone to let him in. It was pretty standard to give contractors keys if they were helping us in the warehouse, but Valentine didn't know that. I had no problem giving one to Doctor Key, but I didn't trust Valentine in my warehouse.

"Sorry, rules," I said, unlocking the door.

Killian and I still shared our telepathic bond, even with his body back.

"You'd better spread the word among the staff to keep that and the grimoire a secret."

"Sasha knows. She's dating Graham, so he knows. If Graham knows, then everyone does."

"Good point. I guess his gossiping is good for something."

"He's one of our best tour guides because he gives them like he's gossiping with his girlfriends. But, he's not malicious about it."

Killian started unpacking breakfast and slid a bento box over to Key.

"Ooh. I grabbed something quick at the hotel, but I require a lot of calories. Thanks."

I'll bet he did. He was massive, and I saw how much he ate when he cooked for us. I was glad Killian included him because I felt more and more like he was one of us.

"Where's mine?" Valentine demanded.

"I'm not your bloody servant," Killian said, biting into his scone.

"Clearly, you're just insecure that Ravyn is going to come back to me."

Killian started choking on his scone. I realized he was laughing. I'd *never* heard him laugh that hard in my entire life, and Ripley and I definitely had our fun at the academy. I was trying so hard not to join him. There was an insecure man baby in this room, and it wasn't Killian.

I processed a few things when I found out Valentine was coming back. His cheating didn't have a damned thing to do with me. He probably did that to countless women. Valentine created this entire persona about the dashing, exciting archaeologist he plagiarized from the Indiana Jones movies to draw women to him.

I was sure I wasn't the only one who fell for it, but he did it because he wanted pretty women hanging on his every word and telling him he was special. So I guessed he had some mommy issues, and she didn't have his back when he got booted from his pack.

"These scones are divine. I'd leave the warlock alone, Valentine. He's already beaten your ass once, and there are priceless relics in here that could get broken. Don't be stupid. Everyone hates the Cult of the Aether Sisters. People are probably upset with you that you disturbed their resting place. The ones that don't recognize the historical significance of these items. You'd be blackballed if you broke something challenging a warlock over his woman."

Valentine grunted and sulked. Key was pretty much a master at Valentine management. How did he do that, anyway? It wasn't all roses the first time he was here. I *adored* going out. There was nothing better than bumping and grinding in a club or drinking with friends in a shifter bar where the drinks were strong and the live music was banging.

I quickly learned that wasn't an option for dates with Valentine. If he thought I wasn't paying attention to him, he started a fight with someone who he thought had mine instead of him. If someone accidentally splashed his shoes with a drink, he punched them in the face. He ruined my good time vibes at my happy places, starting fights every time we went out.

He certainly wouldn't listen to me when I tried to stop him. He just did it anyway if I asked him not to when we were getting ready to go out. If he wanted to go out, the only safe place seemed to be dinner or movies. That wasn't my favorite date, but I thought it was a better option than not having him in my life at all.

Yeah, I was a little dick stupid. I wasn't proud of it.

How did Key *do* that, anyway? The Valentine I dated would have started a fight with Killian for being in my life. He already did and got his ass beat, but he'd be itching for another one to prove he was stronger than Killian. Valentine had no claim to me. He knew that, but he was still pissed he wasn't the center of my world anymore.

He'd be itching for that. Valentine didn't need to worm his way into any witch's bed to get their help with that grimoire. There were plenty that would sign up for that because the contents were probably dark. It was just how he operated.

Valentine stomped off to an empty table to sulk and watch us eat. There was no spell alive that would bend someone to your will. My sister was dating a god, and I'd met Lilith. The gods seemed pretty big on free will. If Lilith could have mind-controlled her creations into doing what she wanted, my sister never would have been kidnapped, and the Hellhounds would have long been freed.

How was Key doing this? Valentine should have challenged him to a fight by now by all rights.

Valentine was back in my face as soon as we put our boxes away. I was a nice person unless you crossed me. Ripley and I volunteered our time towards plenty of causes because we enjoyed doing it. I went to Hell because someone had kidnapped my sister, but I wasn't complaining about freeing the Hellhounds while we were there.

Being nice to Valentine was just hard. It was more than just what he did to me. He was rude to Killian, and that just pissed me off. Killian was into banter, but he was always kind unless you gave him a reason. I saw him with Key. We still didn't know his first name, but those two were like old friends now.

It felt like hot garbage was oozing down my skin when he touched me. I wanted to vomit on his shoes to get him away from me, then kick him straight in the balls to make sure he stayed away. He didn't creep me out this much before, but his aura wasn't like that the last time he was here. Most sane witches avoided people whose auras did that.

"You never told me what you found in the box, Ravyn."

Key swooped in and saved me. He slammed his hand on the table and left a handful of silver coins.

"Rare Viking currency. The Loki coins never caught on like the other coins depicting the other Norse gods. Back in the heyday of the Norse gods, Loki had a bit of an underground following."

I picked up the coin. It was in pristine condition. Where did he get these?

"That doesn't make sense," Killian said. "Loki was a trickster, but he wasn't evil like the Cult of the Aether Sisters. He did things in his own way, but he seemed pretty helpful when it was needed, at least from what I know of Norse gods."

They started teaching us about the different gods in elementary school. They couldn't teach us magic, so they taught us history, theory, and ethics. They covered most of the popular gods throughout history because one of their creations might be in the classroom.

I didn't say anything because we needed Valentine to believe those coins were in the box. The cult being secret Loki worshippers didn't sound right to me. There were stories of people coming to them for help before they became infamous, and they did the exact opposite of help. Loki caused trouble, but he seemed like he stepped in and got shit done when needed. The Cult of the Aether Sisters wouldn't have been into that.

We just needed Valentine to believe they were and had these coins in a locked box.

"Yes!" he said, picking up the coins. "These are probably worth millions of dollars now. I *know* why they had these. They were planning for the future."

Oh, man. What a dumbass. He didn't go to the Academy

of the Profane like I did, but he still went to an expensive private school growing up and a decent university. He'd been taught about the horrors of the Cult of the Aether Sisters and the mythology behind Loki.

His job involved asking hard questions. Valentine hadn't asked me how I picked that blood lock. The only person who had figured out how to do that was Minerva Krauss. She hadn't published it in any of her books because she didn't want to be responsible for mass robberies. Ripley and I only knew because she gave Ripley her diaries when the whole Dorian Gray thing was going on.

Anyone would have asked how I did it. Valentine *should* have asked. I was certain he came across many of them on his digs that his team wouldn't have been able to open. It would have been difficult for his team without a twin, though it would have been possible if they made it a point to donate blood and save it.

He didn't want to know. He was more concerned about the grimoire. And he just played his hand. He was so in on whatever plot they had to come back, he was going to make sure they were well funded.

Holy shit. Valentine had totally lost the plot, and he chose to do it at my museum.

CHAPTER 19

Killian

I was all for banning Valentine from the museum. He wasn't talking anymore. He was utterly giddy over those Loki coins Key produced. He wanted to take them and have them appraised. This plonker forgot where he was. He signed his loot over to the Museum of the Profane. Valentine wasn't getting a damned dime selling this anywhere.

I didn't trust him with those coins. Key looked like he hated Valentine's grubby paws all over them, and I didn't blame him. Those coins were in better condition than some of the pennies Ravyn and Ripley picked up on the street. The twins used their pendulums like any good witch, but if they weren't rock solid on a decision, a penny would appear on the ground somewhere. Heads up was no. Tails up were yes.

I didn't know where Key got them or why they were in such pristine condition, but if they were mine, I wouldn't want them sold to bankroll a bunch of deranged hybrids. Valentine wasn't talking about anything but those coins. At least his mind was off the grimoire.

"I still think I should take these to be appraised."

"We have an in-house appraiser, but you know none of

these items are for sale, Valentine. They belong to the museum now. You agreed to that when you signed the contract."

"They *belong* to the Cult of the Aether Sisters," Valentine snapped.

Actually, if you wanted to get technical, they belonged to a strange warlock who wouldn't tell us his first name that seemed to know more about literally everything than the smartest witch I knew, spoke fluent Old Norse, and had random obscure coins lying around to trick a werewolf.

"Who are quite dead and reduced to bones in boxes," Key said. "No witch with enough power to *properly* raise that many people are going to do it because it would use up all their magic, and they'd be helpless when the cult came back. And not every witch is trained in necromancy for a good reason. If you ask someone to raise the dead with a video they found online, you're just going to end up with revenants."

Valentine's gaze went straight to Ravyn, and he told on himself. One witch wasn't capable of raising the entire cult without nearly killing themselves. Gemini twins had enough magic if they shared to do it safely. Ripley and Ravyn were so damned Gemini it was painful sometimes. They were both brilliant at necromancy too. Ripley helped people with it at the library and was strong enough to force the God of Chaos back into his vessel when she was tricked.

Valentine collaborated with witches. He knew enough to know twin witches were blessed, and if they happened to be Gemini twins, they were extremely powerful. He knew that, but he clearly didn't know Ravyn and Ripley, despite spending time around both of them. They loved mischief and breaking little rules, but never when it came to their jobs and never anything that would throw off the cosmic balance.

The fact that there was a known god living at the Library of the Profane had been all over the news. Reyson wasn't keeping it a secret either. Balthazar set him up a YouTube channel, and he was now doing shirtless cooking videos. He'd amassed quite a following with that. The *only* reason the Library of the Profane wasn't swarming with paparazzi trying to get photos and quotes from him was that Ripley's library was a little more temperamental than Ravyn's Museum. No one wanted to risk being magically escorted from the library and losing the ability to ever locate it again for a snippet from the God of Chaos.

If he thought he could somehow force both twins to do something against their will, he must be dumber than I thought. They could wonder twin his ass so hard, time would go backwards, and his mom would have made damned sure she had birth control the night she conceived him.

Valentine had better think twice if he had ideas about disabling the twins and trying to force them. *If* he managed to overpower them, Ripley being kidnapped to Hell didn't stop any of us from going to get her. I'd kill him, and I was pretty sure Key would have my back on that. That was *nothing* compared to what Ripley's men would do.

"Don't even think about it, man," Key warned.

Valentine had been obeying Key when it came to things he would usually use his fists for. I recognized that look. He wasn't planning on listening to him about this.

CHAPTER 20

Ravyn

Killian knew damned well I found dangerous relics kinky as Hell. I always wanted to jump right in, and he didn't want me to do it. Conversations were had, and a compromise was always struck. I'd always unravel their mysteries and disable them after taking ten minutes to go through the safety precautions he wanted me to do.

I hadn't died yet, and I hadn't been cursed in a way I didn't know how to remove with his guidance, so I always listened and tried not to get argumentative about it.

Key seemed to want to charge ahead with the puzzle box, but he wasn't my familiar, and I didn't know his first name. So he was just going to have to wait while we did scans on the box. The fact that he wanted to dive straight into this mysterious puzzle box from a dangerous cult with no precautions spoke to my soul on a *very* deep level. However, I managed to get this far listening to Killian, and this was still my museum.

Key seemed to understand that. He backed off and let me do my thing as soon as Killian and I told him what we were doing and why. Valentine was being a turd. He still thought the grimoire was in the puzzle box, so he was sulking all over my warehouse, demanding we hurry up and open it.

He wasn't about to try himself. He wanted the three witches in the room to risk it. Fuck him.

Sasha was scanning the grimoire and sending the pages to Killian and me. I asked her to include Key because I trusted him with that information. If he wanted that grimoire to do harm with it, he knew where it was. He seemed more concerned with keeping it away from bad people.

We spent the rest of the week cataloging the rest of the items Valentine found. They were pretty tame, considering the history of the cult. The ornate athames were expected. There were jars of herbs and some crystals. Unfortunately, the wooden effigies of gods were too damaged to tell who they were, and Key didn't have the answer for that like he did everyone else.

I was glad when the weekend came. Valentine was getting on my last nerve, and we couldn't do a lot of what we needed with him hovering in the warehouse. We *should* have been working as a team with one of us translating the grimoire while the rest of us were working, but we couldn't let him know we had it.

I was stressed because he was fucking up my work groove. I needed a break, and brunch with my twin to teach Beyla a little magic was perfect. Killian and I drove to the library. I was actually regretting not inviting Key. He just meshed well with Killian and me, and there was probably a lot he could teach a young witch.

Still, he hadn't asked me a single thing about Reyson. People knew he was at the library and dating my sister now. They wouldn't come here in person, but people had called both of us for statements. News outlets who I gave interviews with plenty of times about exhibits bothered me about my twin's boyfriend until they realized I wasn't going to spill dirt about my sister. Even my friends that knew damned well I never gossiped about my twin had texted.

So, why hadn't Key asked me anything? He knew Reyson was there. He seemed to have this thirst for knowledge, but he didn't want to know about either god I'd met. Since he was a warlock, he probably had a million questions about Lilith, but he never asked me.

Beyla was already sitting with Ripley, Felix, and Gabriel. Bram, Balthazar, and Reyson must have dragged Kaine away for some man bonding. I joined them at the table with my basket. I didn't have kids, and I probably wouldn't for a long time, so it was exciting to make a witchy care package for someone.

I slid the basket over, and Beyla peered inside.

"Okay, my parents didn't have any of this stuff lying around the house. They had herbs for cooking, but I don't recognize most of this."

"Even those herbs have their uses. They might not have had any obvious signs of witchcraft around the house, but there are plenty of kitchen witches who do their own magic with spices and intention," Killian said.

"So, I'm not just a witch. I have to pick what kind of witch I want to be?"

"Girl, the beauty of being a witch is that you don't have to choose a damned thing," Ripley said. "I had five hot guys in my library, and I didn't have to choose then either. You're *expected* to learn whatever magic strikes your fancy and form a strong coven. Some witches love a certain kind of magic and like to put a name on themselves, but a good bit of us just call ourselves witches and do what we want."

"I don't even know where to start. I'm having nightmares after everything that happened, and sometimes, I'm tripping the breaker at Kaine's house when I don't mean to."

"That's why you need to protect yourself," I said. "We're

going to teach you protection spells today. It's the first thing any witch should learn."

"We're going to teach you to make a spell jar you need to bury in Kaine's yard. It'll protect both of you," Ripley said,

Beyla started worrying her bottom lip with her teeth.

"Kaine is really anal about his lawn. So is his neighborhood of dragons. They all seemed to be really into gold, but there's this entire competition about their yards. All Kaine talks about sometimes is how he came in second place last year, and he just has to win this year, or he'll literally die. I had less anxiety about my ballet school audition."

Modern dragons were so weird. There used to be a time they took pride in their caves and hordes. They couldn't exactly run amok plundering gold from kings in their dragon forms anymore. They didn't get into fights over the best cave space that would keep their treasures from being stolen or dragon hunters finding them. They lived in the suburbs now and were obsessed with their lawns and gold.

"You don't have to explain Kaine's obsession with his grass to us," I said. "It doesn't have to be buried in a place that messes it up. I know he has a very nice garden too and wouldn't mind you burying this there if it means you are safe."

Kaine was pretty gruff unless it came to Beyla. She was his weak spot. I knew he wanted to win that lawn competition, but if she needed to dig a massive hole in his front yard to keep bad people from hurting her, Kaine would let her.

Gabriel whipped out a piece of parchment and some charcoal. He slid it over to Beyla. We all knew what he wanted her to do, but her parents kept so much of her birthright from her, she didn't know.

"I'm shit at art. I've been able to easily do the thirty-two *fouettés* from Swan Lake for years, but I can barely draw a stick figure. Do I have to be good at art and ballet too if I'm going to be a witch?"

"Not at all," Killian said. "Sigil work isn't about being perfect. It's about intention. You'll need to practice this in addition to your ballet when your feet heal. You close your eyes, center yourself, and visualize your intention. Let your hand move, and it will draw the sigil. If it doesn't speak to you when you open your eyes, just do it again until you draw one that does. When you start getting your sigils down, you'll want to record them in your grimoire."

"I got you a blank one to use for now, but we'll have to take you shopping for the one you are going to keep and pass down. You should pick the one that speaks to you," I said.

"I'm guessing they aren't made from human skin and written in blood like they say in the human world?"

"What the actual fresh hell?" I said. "I've got countless grimoires at the museum, and none of them are like that."

Even the Cult of the Aether Sister's grimoire wasn't bound in human skin and written in blood. Humans were just so *weird*. Literally, no one was doing that. Beyla just shrugged.

"I like horror movies. That's what they do in those movies."

"We're going to have to introduce you to supernatural streaming channels because they have much more accurate horror movies," Felix said.

"Oh, I know. Kaine and I watch them together. He calls it a working education."

That was kind of adorable. Kaine around Beyla was adorable. Dragons were fiercely loyal to their families and would do anything to protect them, but they mostly kept to themselves and didn't mix with the other supernatural races. Kaine treated Beyla like she was his whelp, but he was a little out of his element.

"Okay, so you know how Kaine was in Hell recently?" Gabriel said. "We were there with him, and we learned demon magic lies in their sigils. They had them tattooed on their skin.

Bram has them hidden in his tattoos. Lilith created witches, demons, and Hellhounds, so we're all related in a way. Witch's magic is different, but we do share a few things, like the sigils. Our sigils can't bring someone's darkest wish to life like a demon, but they are still potent. Why don't you try?"

"I think they are teaching this to the witches at my new high school, but because of my history, they stuck me in remedial classes with all the burnouts. I was a straight-A student at my old high school. I'm so behind now."

"Between Kaine and us, we'll have you caught up in no time. The other students aren't being stupid, are they?" I asked.

"I'm not supposed to talk about being raised human. They think it's cool I'm a dancer and think I focus on that instead of school, and that's why I'm in remedial classes. A few people have offered me drugs, and some thought I was selling them."

Felix looked completely amused by this.

"Did you tell Kaine?"

"Oh, shit, no. He'd show up at my high school and roast someone with dragon fire. I'd *never* get a date to prom after that. I don't really want to date again after Derrick, but I don't mind using someone for arm candy for the memories."

I *really* liked this kid and fully supported her men ban until she found one that wasn't physically abusive and supportive of her ballet career. I wasn't a dancer, but I loved watching it. I knew about the company whose school Beyla had auditioned for because they had donated items to my museum.

I spoke to them at length about the history behind them, and I knew exactly what dancers put themselves through to get into companies like that. The fact that Beyla's boyfriend was willing to take all that away from her by breaking both of her feet still astounded me.

Before Beyla could practice her sigils, Reyson did that thing he liked to do where he appeared out of nowhere. He'd brought Kaine, Balthazar, and Bram with him, and they all had trays of food. I'd forgotten all about brunch, and I was starving.

Beyla didn't seem to be one of those dancers that restricted her food, and Kaine wasn't pressuring her to eat. She fixed herself a plate of options that would keep her body fueled if she had a day of dancing after this. She had a good head on her, and with our help, she'd be in the advanced classes at her high school in no time.

Reyson kept staring at Beyla, which meant he was up to something, and there was a fifty percent chance whatever came out of his mouth was going to get Kaine to set his ass on fire.

"What do the modern healers say about your feet?"

"They said even with the physical therapy after the casts come off, dancing may always be painful."

"I could heal your feet as if they were never broken. Then, you could go back to doing what brings you joy."

Reyson could be epically weird sometimes, but I got what my sister saw in him. He'd destroy the cosmos for my twin, but he also did good things because it was just who he was. I doubted Reyson would bring back her parents or could find her dickhead ex-boyfriend, but he could make it possible for her to dance again.

"I'd love that more than anything, but what would I tell people who know my feet are broken?"

"It's not a secret I'm here anymore. So tell them you know me," Reyson said.

Okay, my sister's boyfriend did some pretty amazing things, but he could have a god sized ego sometimes.

"I'm not worried about the people at my high school. They are used to magic. It's the humans that know me. Some of my human friend's parents have been bothering Kaine for taking me in because they don't know him. Derrick disappeared, and his parents think I had something to do with it. They are practically stalking me and showing up at random places demanding to know what I did with him. If they see me without my casts this early, they'll start saying I made up him breaking my feet."

"No. No way," Kaine said. "I'm tired of that boy and his family dictating your life when he possibly ended your dance career. He's still doing it long after he fucked off somewhere he can't be punished for what he did to you. His parents are seriously deranged if they think you could have murdered him with two broken feet and disappeared his body the same night you were in the hospital. If you absolutely feel the need to keep up appearances, let Reyson heal you, but we can manipulate those casts, so you only have to wear them in public."

"I can do that too," Reyson said.

"Don't let them win, Beyla," Killian said. "I'm not sure where their deranged crotch fruit disappeared to after he abused you, but I know what kind of people they are. They *want* your dance career to be over because they think he's the victim here."

"Well, I certainly didn't do it, but what if he was? His parents gave him everything he wanted. If he were going to run, they would have been in on it. They would have set him up somewhere with money, a place to live, and probably a new car."

"Witching 101," I said. "Karma and fate are major for us. He had some threefold shit coming his way for possibly ending your dance career, and he probably would have hurt other women after you."

"Yeah, but I have magic now. I didn't when he hurt me. I have things I want to say to him, and I want to watch him feel as helpless as I felt that night. Someone took that away from me. Please, heal my feet. They aren't taking ballet away too."

I smiled while Reyson took care of her feet and casts. Her parents may have tried to keep her from her birthright, but that kid was *definitely* a witch.

CHAPTER 21

Killian

By the time we left lunch, little Beyla wasn't just walking around perfectly. She gave us a ballet performance in the garden after we begged her when she said it was like they were never broken. That kid was going to be a famous prima ballerina one day.

Her magic was still raw, but she weaved an enchantment while she was dancing. She was just improvising to music on Ripley's cell phone, but she was good. And some stupid teenage boy nearly took that from her because he was threatened by it. Thank Lilith for Reyson that he could give her dance career back to her if she wanted it.

Ravyn and I were back at her cottage, looking at the scans from the grimoire. I had a lot of things to say about the evil shit the Cult of the Aether Sisters got up to, but their grimoire was absolutely beautiful. Someone had taken the time and care to illustrate it with the plants and crystals needed for the spells.

Ravyn and I could translate this, but it would take time, and we couldn't exactly do it at the museum with Valentine there. I was just as work focused as Ravyn was, especially now that I had more options for helping her at the museum. Valentine was ruining that.

There was a lot of pretty obvious innuendo at brunch to know Ripley abused dating a god and asked him to look at Ravyn's love life. I got that Ripley was happy, and she wanted that for her twin, but this was important and couldn't be forced. Still, if Reyson saw a coven forming, I actually liked Key and got along with him. Ravyn liked him too. I'd never pressure her like Ripley was doing. But, technically, we *needed* his help.

"Do you think Key would want to come over on his day off if we bribed him with your good whiskey? The grimoire is massive, and we can't translate it with Valentine all up in our business. Sasha has sent us twenty pages so far, and neither of us is as good with Old Norse as Key."

"I don't know if I should be annoyed or impressed, he knows things I don't and can translate ancient runes like he's reading some of the fiction at Ripley's library."

"Bitch, you're lying if you're trying to say you aren't utterly impressed that he's brilliant, and it doesn't turn you on a little that he could just look at these scans and tell you exactly what they say."

Fuck, I wasn't even remotely bisexual, and it turned *me* on. Intelligence was sexy. Yeah, a pretty face was nice, but if you couldn't have conversations that challenged you, what was the point? Ravyn was the full package, and so was Key. I'd like to think I fit in there, too, somewhere.

"Okay, it *is* sexy. It's his day off, though."

"I get the feeling that warlock doesn't do a damned thing he doesn't want to do. He didn't bulldoze his way onto Valentine's dig to share his knowledge or end up quoted in books and articles. Key came because of that prophesy and the upcoming eclipse. He's not like Valentine. Key *wants* to stop it. If the answer to that is in the grimoire, I think he would be mad not to be invited. Plus, I get the feeling he finds translating ancient grimoires just as sexy as we do."

"Probably so, and that speaks to my soul."

"So, call him and invite him over. We're going to need all the help we can get. Valentine knows how the cult plans to use the eclipse to come back, but he's not going to tell you with us in the room and until he thinks you're going to help him."

"Good call. I'm all about whipping out the magic vagina to manipulate the villain because they are generally stupid like that, but Valentine's aura is giving me the creeps."

Valentine was giving all of us the creeps with that nasty aura of his. If Reyson saw the possibilities of Ravyn forming her own coven, now was definitely the time for it.

CHAPTER 22

Raryn

I was nervous about calling Key. I wanted him here, and he just fit in so well with Killian and me. I broke my rule about getting involved with coworkers with Valentine, and it hadn't worked out that great for me. Key was fucking brilliant. He'd make an amazing consultant for my museum when this was over. Key had a home somewhere, and he had mentioned nothing about loving this town so much, he wanted to uproot and move here.

Key picked up on the first ring.

"I'm epically bored. Save me before I get arrested again."

"What did you get arrested for the first time?" I asked.

"I was bored, and some people overreacted. They could never make the charges stick."

"Well, we can't have you getting arrested now, can we? Want to come over and get drunk with us while translating a deranged cult's grimoire?"

"That depends. Are you going to get kinky when you think I'm not paying attention and do birth control magic literally right next to me?"

I had just taken a sip of my tea when he said that and spat

it right at Killian. I joked I hoped he noticed, but now that I knew he had, I wanted to crawl up my own asshole and die. I could hear him laughing as I choked on my tea.

"I'm all about safe sex, Ravyn. I hope you put it to use and had a good time. I'd love to come. Unfortunately, I'm a hangry drunk, so we'll probably have to order a big greasy pizza later. Do you need me to bring anything?"

"Just that sexy ass of yours."

Fuck. Why did I say that? I pretty much said shit like that to men all the time before my dick exile, but never people I worked with. You had to have a twisted sense of humor to work at any of the Profane buildings. The buildings were all haunted as fuck. Ripley's ghosts were mostly well behaved, but some of her books bit. It took a special kind of crazy to teach eighteen-year-olds who just had their magic awakened at the Academy of the Profane. The vampires were the only ones who had been living with everything since they were kids. Students went a little nuts.

Then, there was my museum. The spirits on these grounds liked to prank us when they weren't having fun with academy students. We had some ancient dildos the board liked to pretend were something else that always ended up in someone's coffee cup if they didn't use one with a lid. We had cameras everywhere and knew damned well it was ghosts trying to flavor people's coffee with ancient vaginas.

Our interior designer, who had been here forever and staged our exhibits, got a coffee mug from her grandkids every Yule. She was the only one of us who hadn't switched to lidded tumblers for coffee or tea. She repeatedly said she refused to negotiate with terrorists every time she fished a dildo out of her coffee.

We made inappropriate jokes among the staff all the time because of some of the things housed in this museum, and it was just who we were, but we never got sexual. Sasha and

Graham were my only employees dating each other, and no one even knew until they pulled me aside and asked my permission for a work relationship. Everyone knew now, but even they weren't as obvious as what I just said to Key.

"I like this side of you. You should do it more often. Don't let that stupid wolf suppress you anymore."

"Sorry, that was totally inappropriate."

"Why? I *know* my ass is sexy. You should touch it. It's nice and firm too."

"Just get over here."

Key laughed.

"Will do, but it's your day off, young witch. Work rules don't apply."

Key liked this side of me, and I rather liked this side of him. I had a feeling everyone at my cottage tonight was going to find translating the grimoire a little sexy, and we were going to be drinking.

I was in so much trouble.

CHAPTER 23

Ravyn

T thought I was mentally prepared for this until Key knocked on my front door. He usually dressed impeccably at the museum, and this fucker showed up at my place in *gray fucking sweatpants* and a tight black T-shirt. That was just playing dirty.

Killian wasn't much better. He looked *glorious* in baggy black jeans with chains and a black muscle shirt. My resolve was weakening. How had I sworn off men for so long? Oh, yeah. I hadn't met any as fascinating as Key, and Killian was stuck as a bat before.

Key thrust a bottle at me before I let him inside. I looked down at the label, and my eyes bugged out of my head. There was a pack of shifters in Ireland who had been making whiskey forever. There were limited batches, and it had a cult following. It was nearly impossible to get a bottle of this whiskey. People put their names on the waiting list and ended up dying before they got a bottle. And supernaturals lived much longer than humans.

"How in actual fuck did you manage to snag this?"

"Barter. I once did a favor for the pack, and now I get a

bottle from every batch. I can't think of any two people I'd like to crack this bottle open with more."

"Are you serious? Hasn't someone been stabbed over this whiskey?" Killian asked.

Key just shrugged.

"In all fairness, people have been stabbed over watered down, shitty whiskey in dirty pubs all over the world."

"That's true," Killian said as we moved to my living room.

Key had a briefcase with him. He didn't usually bring one to the museum. He set it on my coffee table and opened it. Key took a book out and slid it towards Killian and me.

"I was going to give this to you once I got all the scans, and Valentine wasn't around."

It was a pretty ornate book. There was nothing on the cover except beautiful gold work that looked a little Viking. I could see someone picking this as a grimoire. When I opened the cover, Key had already translated the pages he had received so far, but he didn't stop there. He'd started illustrating it like the cult's grimoire.

I always wanted one of those beautifully illustrated grimoires like we got in the museum, but drawing had never been a strength of mine. Shit, the Cult of the Aether Sisters had members that drew better than I did. Key was also an amazing artist. He had the line work down on the first page and even did borders.

"This is beautiful," I said, stroking the vellum.

Key just shrugged like it was no big deal.

"I told you. I'm trying not to get arrested again. I need to be at the museum to help stop Valentine. These are just doodles."

He wasn't just saying that to be modest. He had a pretty healthy ego when he wanted to. Key really was bored when he wasn't at the museum, so he drew in this book and didn't think it was a big deal. I was pretty amazed at his drawings, but

I didn't want to make him uncomfortable. Though, I doubted that might be possible.

"You know you can always come here if you're bored. Just leave Valentine at the hotel."

I saw his facade crack a little. He looked grateful for the invitation. Was he lonely here? Did he know anyone?

"I'd like that. Anyway, these are mostly healing potions so far. The cult didn't start out bad. They twisted into something evil later."

Killian and I leaned over the book and took in the potions and salves in here. There was one for burns the rest of the world hadn't seen. Most of the burn remedies we used now had aloe in them. This one didn't. I didn't even know what some of these herbs were.

"What is this, and how does it treat burns?" I asked.

"They lanced wounds a good bit. There wasn't much treatment for the burn. This is a psychotropic tea. I guess if you are hallucinating, you can't feel it. There are some potions for coughs and salves for rashes in here so far."

"These are all for healing. Aren't there stories of people going to them for medical remedies and getting potions that either killed them or made them worse?" Killian asked.

"Yes, but that doesn't mean they didn't *have* working remedies or give them out at first. How fast can your girl get us the rest of the grimoire?"

"Sasha is an amazing worker, and she's good at what she does. She's getting us the pages as quickly as she can without damaging the grimoire," I said.

"What about the puzzle box?"

"We've finished all the scans. We can't identify what's at the center," Killian said. "It's obviously magic, but nothing we've ever seen before. It could be the magic they need to come back during the eclipse. They *have* to know that no one would be insane enough to raise them with necromancy."

"There's not a lot of them out there, but there *are* seers. They were revered next to gods in the past, and any successful group of people out there had one close to them. The few that exist now tend to view it as a curse and don't get involved in people's business. This prophecy came from a seer, but visions are never whole. It's always snippets. At most, they knew the upcoming eclipse was vital, but not *how*.

"Witches are able to raise the dead and commune with spirits because Lilith made you that way. The only beings capable of doing that are gods and witches. The Cult of the Aether Sisters weren't witches. They wouldn't have the same mastery over the spirits as one. They weren't in power long enough to cook up something that would beat good old-fashioned necromancy. They converted Valentine. It's not a huge stretch he'd find friends out there willing to help."

I'd never personally met a seer, but I knew Lilith had created those too. The only reason I knew that was because Bram told my sister he lived with one when he stayed with Talvath. Key was right. Talvath held his seer in high regard, and so did Bram. But he rarely left Talvath's house because of his visions.

Killian made some good points too. There was a gigantic mass of magic at the center of that puzzle box that none of our high-tech scanners could identify. If Key knew what it was, he wasn't telling us. Also, the craftsmanship on the puzzle box was way too advanced for that era. It didn't match anything else from the dig or anything else in my museum from that time period.

I still wanted to open it.

"What if this box didn't belong to the cult?" I asked. "There's no damage to it from the fire, and there are mechanical gears on the scans. Those definitely weren't around then."

"Valentine didn't plant it when he was alone at the ruins," Killian said. "He seems pretty convinced the grimoire is in there. I agree, though. The Cult of the Aether Sisters didn't have the technology available to make this box."

"The god that made them would have," I said. "They didn't step in when the cult got dangerous. We saw how Lilith was with her creations. She let the demons abuse the Hellhounds for ages, so she didn't have to go on a killing spree. Gods seem pretty protective of their creations. Whoever created them could have made them this box to help the prophecy come true."

"We've spent more time around Reyson than we did Lilith. They are both totally different. If Reyson had created a supernatural race and they went evil, he'd step in. If there were any chance of them coming back, he'd make sure to stop it. Gods are just as different as we are. There could be answers about who created them and how to stop them inside the puzzle box."

"Something isn't sitting right with me. The cult spoke to Valentine enough to convert him to their evil plan. *He* doesn't know what's in that puzzle box. Valentine is convinced the grimoire is in there. Maybe the Cult of the Aether Sisters doesn't know what's in the box either. If it were vital to their plans, they would have told him."

"Or Valentine is lying," Killian pointed out.

"I don't think so," Key said. "Valentine needs the grimoire. They told him it was in a box. They weren't very specific. Valentine is not very sneaky. He hasn't revealed all of his plans because he knows Ravyn isn't on his side, but he's told us a good bit of it."

"So, it's settled," Killian said. "Monday, we open the box."

Key stretched.

"I'm at the point that I'd like that pizza now. Unless I've worn out my welcome?"

He hadn't. I enjoyed having him here. I wanted Key here more often. I wouldn't want him to get arrested or anything.

CHAPTER 24

Ravyn

We were epically drunk, and I was having a blast. I was fluent in modern drinking games. Killian and Key were breaking out games I hadn't even heard of. Key stood up and stretched. His body was doing things in those gray sweatpants that were speaking to my soul. He placed an empty beer bottle in the center of my coffee table and looked deadly serious.

"It is now time for the most important drinking game of all time—spin the bottle."

I hadn't played that since the academy and Key and Killian were so damned hot, it was probably unfair to the female species. I was here for that.

"How are we going to play spin the bottle? There are only three of us here and only one woman," Killian said.

Key just winked at him. If Killian and Key kissed, my vagina might explode.

"There's not a damned thing wrong with two men kissing."

"Oh, I know. I've just never wanted to."

"Well, it's two in the morning, we've gone through most of a bottle of rare whiskey, and it's the perfect time to experiment."

Killian must have either been really drunk or just a little curious because he pointed his slice of pizza at Key and grunted.

"You'd better not slip me the tongue."

"Both of you have my full permission to slip me the tongue," I said.

Yeah, this whiskey was potent and making me pretty bold, but I wasn't smashed. That wasn't the whiskey talking. Killian was an amazing kisser, and I'd been looking at Key in those gray sweatpants all night. I'll bet he kissed like a total beast.

"Noted. I'm the oldest, so I'll go first," Key said.

How did he *know* he was the oldest? We never discussed birthdays, and he looked our age. He'd somehow managed to guess Killian was my familiar. We hadn't confirmed that even though we probably should. When Reyson brought Killian back, he brought him back in his prime, but he remembered his life from before. Key couldn't be older than Killian, but we just went with it.

I was pretty sure Killian felt the same as I did. We could be honest with Key about what he was and how he got that way. I knew he wouldn't share that information with anyone and cause some sort of rebellion among the familiars or a mob at my sister's library. He seemed to know a lot about generally everything and a very curious warlock. But he never shared anything he knew unless it helped someone.

I opened my mouth to point out Killian was technically older than him and give Key the truth, but he was already spinning the beer bottle. That was totally Key. He just said anything and did what he wanted. It was mostly directed towards shitting on Valentine, but it was still extremely sexy.

136

The bottle landed on Killian. Killian bit his lower lip. Killian had been my familiar a very long time. He'd been with Ripley and me while we were checking out guys, and he never wanted to join in. Being stupid hot was never a good reason to him for me being into a guy. I generally agreed with him after I tried to have a conversation with them.

Key was stupid hot, brilliant, and oozed power. He hit everything on my bucket list and at least two on Killian's. He was missing the parts Killian usually went for, but was that curiosity on his face?

It was definitely curiosity. Key grabbed him and just went for it. And there was definitely tongue. It was definitely reciprocated too. This was my new favorite TV show. Key pulled away and sat back down. Killian looked like his entire world had just been rocked.

"Okay, so I'm not sure if I'm into guys or just into you. You have this weird magnetism."

"I know," Key smirked.

"I fully support any experimentations you'd like to do as long as I get to watch," I said.

"Well, I haven't gotten to kiss *you* yet," Key said.

I *finally* felt like myself again, and Ravyn Bell didn't need a bottle's permission to kiss a hot warlock.

"Fuck the bottle," I said, crawling into his lap.

I crashed my lips down on his. I was straddling him and pulling his red hair, but he quickly took control from me. Oh, damn. He was good at this. I was officially turned on. How long had it been since my last *good* threesome? I already knew Killian was a beast in bed. If Key kissed like that, I knew they could rock a warlock sandwich.

"We should so take this back to my bedroom."

"Fuck yes," Killian growled.

Key wrapped his arms around me and stood up like I

weighed nothing. I hoped he used that strength to throw me around the bedroom a little bit because I was in a mood. He bit my earlobe.

"Lead the way, my good friend."

Killian

What in actual fuck was happening? This wasn't my first threesome with another man. I'd been to orgies where the men outnumbered the women. I'd never remotely been interested in kissing another guy until Key wanted to play spin the bottle like we were still in university.

I was against the idea at first. Then, I started thinking about it. Key was insanely attractive. I could admit that. We got along great. What generally grabbed my attention in women was intelligence and power. I respected the crap out of Ravyn and her sister because they had this massive thirst for knowledge and were always seeking it out.

Key was like that too, and he didn't really have a damned thing to prove about it either. He wasn't acting superior that he had all this knowledge about the cult that we didn't. Illustrated grimoires were highly coveted, even now. People paid a ton of money for that. Key illustrated the translations because he was bored and didn't think it was a huge deal.

Why *wouldn't* I at least be curious about what kissing him was like?

It was pretty much amazing. And having a threesome where you could kiss everyone was even better. I couldn't have done this with just anyone. I guess I was attracted to the person, and I hadn't met any men I wanted to do this with before.

And I loved sharing this moment with Ravyn. This was a vulnerable moment for me. I was opening myself up to something I'd never done before. Ravyn and Key were making this totally perfect. Ravyn was all over Key and me. Key pleasured Ravyn and was totally courteous of me never doing this before.

He let me explore his body and only touched me where I touched him. I appreciated that because I honestly didn't know what my limits were. I really enjoyed kissing him. Key's skin was amazingly soft. I was all about modern beauty products. I needed to find out what he was using.

I buried my face in Ravyn's breasts while Key stroked my cock. I slipped my hand between her legs and rubbed slow circles on her clit.

"Okay, I need both of you right now."

I was pretty sure I knew what Ravyn had in mind, and she hated being told what to do. Key decided to take control, anyway.

"I think I'd like to watch Killian take you from behind with that impressive cock while you suck mine."

"Or you could put me in a hot, warlock sandwich," Ravyn purred.

Key tucked her hair behind her ear and smiled.

"I don't think you're quite ready for that yet, little witch. I'm guessing Valentine wasn't into sharing when you were with him. You said you swore off men until Killian somehow turned human. So you shouldn't go for the full double stuff on your first threesome. Baby steps."

"But I want the double stuff," Ravyn sulked.

Ravyn didn't do baby steps. She never had. The only reason she wasn't in jail was because she had me, and Minerva Krauss took her under her wing. Ripley was usually up for it, but sometimes she had to talk Ravyn down too. She knew what she wanted right now, and she usually got it. This time, it wasn't illegal, so I fully had her back on this.

"I know you do. And we will. Just not tonight."

What was his deal? I didn't know any man on the planet that would say no to what Ravyn wanted, and that hadn't changed since the last time I was alive. Key kissed the tip of her nose.

"Please? I'd like to watch you and Killian while feeling your mouth. It would mean a lot to me."

I wasn't going to say no to that, and neither would Ravyn. For whatever reason, Key wanted it a certain way, and neither of us was into kink shaming. And his idea was completely sexy too. No one would be left out.

Key was massive. I was an excellent fighter and had taken down men twice my size, but it would have been really hard to disable Key. Ravyn pounced and shoved him on his back. I taught her everything she knew about fighting, but Key dramatically fell back like either of us was his size.

Ravyn pounced on his cock and started waving her perfect arse at me. I wasn't about to say no to that. Now that Ravyn decided she was ready, we had a pretty healthy sex life. We were learning to please each other and experimenting with different kinks and positions, but we hadn't tried this one yet.

Ravyn had this exquisite back. Key wasn't the only one getting a show. I had a full view of Ravyn pleasuring Key. I grasped my cock and guided it inside her. Ravyn let out this huge moan. She made the best sex noises. Key was showing his gratitude, and his weren't bad either. Time for me to do my part.

She enjoyed it hard and fast, but I liked to build up to that.

Any asshole could sit there pounding away like a caveman. No one liked that. It probably chafed like a bitch. But, if you worked up to it, you lasted longer, and so did she.

When I had her right where I wanted her, I leaned forward and started rubbing her clit. Key was pulling her hair, and I knew she loved that too. I'd experienced Ravyn's oral skills. Key was enjoying them just as much as I did.

Shit. This was just so fucking hot. Ravyn wasn't the only one who hadn't done this in a while. Hers was just a few years, but mine was much longer. We both needed this, and I think we were both happy it was happening with Key.

I fluttered my fingers on her clit faster. Her cries were muffled around Key's cock. I let go when I felt her clamp down on my cock. Based on the noises he was making, Key did too. Holy shit. I would *never* tire of doing this with Ravyn, and I hope Key was more involved too.

We collapsed in a heap on her bed and snuggled into Ravyn.

"Stay the night," Ravyn said. "Please don't leave."

I didn't really want him to leave either. It just felt right having him here. Key kissed the top of her head.

"I'd love to sleep snuggling with you. If Killian doesn't fight me, I'll cook breakfast for both of you."

"I'm all about one of us spoiled Ravyn."

"Yeah, but I was going to spoil you too."

That was kind of nice. Of course, it would be great to be spoiled a little. I didn't regret kissing him at all.

CHAPTER 26

Raryn

Key spent the night and never left. I wasn't even mad about that. Even though I fell for Valentine's bull-shit, he annoyed the shit out of me in my personal space full time. It wasn't like that with Key or even Killian, for that matter. I hadn't met anyone I wanted to cohabitate with until Killian. It just happened with Key, and it didn't annoy me, so I didn't kick him out of my house.

Key was a little weird about sex. As in, all we did was lots of oral. I wasn't complaining because it was amazing, but I wanted to experience the D because he had a pretty one. Key was pretty much amazing helping Killian explore his newfound bisexuality, and that just made me like him more.

I'd honestly forgotten all about Valentine until we walked to the museum, and he was standing there all scowly, waiting for us.

"I knocked on your door for thirty straight minutes. I tried to find you at the hotel all weekend. So you were fucking my woman this entire time? Is bro code not sacred to you?"

"Okay, bro code is just an asinine set of rules to excuse toxic behavior. If you actually cared about it, you wouldn't have cheated on Ravyn. You would have cheated with her twin if you could have gotten away with it," Key growled.

"I didn't cheat on Ravyn. We were on pause. And I never would have cheated with her twin. Riley scares me."

"Ripley!" I yelled. "Her name is Ripley. This is the second time I've told you this!"

"It's not a pause if both people aren't aware of it, you arse," Killian said.

"Is that why you're so mad at me, baby? Didn't you know we were on pause? You don't need these two. I know I'm better in bed than either of them. Get rid of them. It can just be you and me like it's supposed to be."

We all rolled our eyes so hard, it probably caused brain damage. Key just came out of nowhere and punched Valentine in the head. Valentine was a big guy, though nowhere near as big as Key. Valentine flew a little and landed on his back. He didn't move.

A big fat raindrop landed on my cheek. I straightened my hair, but if it got wet, it would frizz to all shit.

"Damn. My hair," I said, swiping my key.

We all rushed inside and just left Valentine outside. I didn't feel sorry for him. He had some weird definition of pausing. First of all, he never mentioned that to me when he left. He made it seem like he'd stay in touch, and we'd have visits at the museum and in other countries.

If he thought pause meant he was free to fuck who he wanted, then he needed to get off my ass about Killian and now Key.

We spread our breakfast out and ate, just ignoring that Valentine was knocked the fuck out on the grass outside. I looked over to Key.

"Thank you for that. It was beautiful to watch."

Key just shrugged.

"He had it coming."

Killian broke into *The Cellblock Tango* from *Chicago*. We both loved that song. I jumped up, and we danced around the warehouse, singing at the top of our lungs. I used to do that all over my cottage with him singing in my head. It was so nice to have him dancing with me in person.

"Fosse would be proud," Key said when we finished.

Supernaturals had their own movies and television shows, but they sometimes performed things humans came up with.

"You should see *Chicago* with an all succubus cast. It's superb," I said.

"I have a soft spot for the madness that is musical theatre. In any other situation, if someone started singing and dancing in the middle of a pub, mortal enemies would come together to kick their asses. Put it on a stage with a name on it, and people wait outside for will-call tickets for sold-out shows. I tip my hat to the madman who created them," Key said.

"We just broke into random song," Killian pointed out. "It happens."

"To celebrate me punching Valentine in the face and leaving him out in the rain. Utter madness. I love it."

"Well, we have two options now. Valentine is either going to go home and sulk, and we'll have a whole day without him, or he's going to come back in here and start a fight."

I'd lay odds he was going to come storming in here getting shit wet and breaking things. I was the only person here who hadn't assaulted Valentine yet. I was feeling a little left out. We didn't even allow running in the museum, much less fistfights from jealous wolves. I would blast his ass if he did.

"He won't," Key said. "I've observed Valentine in the wild. He usually only picks fights he thinks he can win. Thinks being the operative word. If he gets his ass handed to him, he slinks off and doesn't show his face again. He knows Killian, and I can best him, but he can't stay away because he needs that grimoire."

"Is it bad I was kind of hoping he came back looking for a fight? I'd like to kick his ass too."

"Patience, little witch. I'm sure you'll get your turn," Key said.

The sad thing was, he was probably right. Why did I even tolerate that before? I was just going to claim temporary insanity on that one. When I did get my chance, it was going to be epic. Maybe if I burned his ass hairs off with a little magic, he'd get it through his head I was pissed and not going back there with him.

"What should we do with our Valentine free day? I really want to hit him every time he gets up in Ravyn's personal space."

"The puzzle box," Key and I said at the same time.

If we could get this thing open while he was off sulking, we could close it back up and pretend like the grimoire was still in there when we closed it back up. It would buy us time while we pretended to run more tests on it before we opened the box.

I didn't know what was in that box. I wasn't even sure what fresh hell would come out of it if we got the answer to one of the puzzles wrong.

I was ass crazy excited to start guessing, though.

CHAPTER 27

Killian

I loved magical puzzle boxes, but in this case, I felt like Brad Pitt in that movie I watched with the twins in high school, and we probably really didn't want to know what was inside. If it was a severed head, I was going to get mad. That was one thing I liked about this century. They didn't behead people anymore and put their heads on spikes to try to deter people from committing crimes. Honestly, I was *over* seeing severed heads.

Puzzle boxes were all the rage back in my time. We didn't have television. The class system was pretty much all the rage back then, and the one I was born into thought plays were for degenerates. At least, the *fun* kind of plays. If you got invited to a party with someone with a lot of money and a fancy title, they put on what they thought was an appropriate show.

It was generally other rich people dressed in costume pretending to be gods and goddesses. Naturally, they tended to favor the Greek gods, even though not a damned one of them created any of us.

We had to find other ways of entertaining ourselves. Women got to do all kinds of fun things like painting and singing. That wasn't really considered appropriate for men, even though I would have loved to learn. I loved puzzle boxes back then, though they weren't quite as intricate as this one and weren't found in the ruins of the boogeyman cult.

Still, I was good at riddles, and so was Ravyn. There didn't seem to be anything Key didn't know, so if there was *ever* a dream team that could figure out this box without dying, it was going to be us.

The first riddle on the box was in Old Nordic runes, but Ravyn and I had seen them enough not to need to reference anything or have Key translate.

"Earth, wind, air, fire?" Ravyn said. "That seems a little easy considering the mass of magic at the center. Any witch can conjure all four elements."

"The Cult of the Aether Sisters weren't witches, though," Key pointed out.

If the cult couldn't summon the elements, then opening this box with the resources available back then would have been next to impossible. They only would have been able to with four witches. Someone might be dumb enough to help them now, but I was pretty sure during their reign of terror, any witch would have fought to the death before helping them.

The entire supernatural community beat them back into their house, and then the witches called fire to set it alight. It burned so hot, the cult didn't have time to flee or fight back, but they had killed plenty of people before they were cornered.

Was this box a weapon against the cult, but they managed to get their hands on it before it could be used? That was the only thing that made sense if the cult couldn't call the elements.

"We need another witch," I said. "I've seen this before on puzzle boxes. It needs to be hit with all four elements at once."

Ravyn set her phone down.

"Already handled. Gabriel is walking over now."

"I heard about that one in the news," Key said. "I hope those judgey assholes the dragon was trying to put in their place have done some ass kissing."

That just endeared Key to me. My contemporaries the last time I was alive were famous for that. No one really cared if you were a terrible person as long as you weren't poor and didn't lose your lands and title. If you lost your head too, they would shun your ancestors for generations.

I didn't know his first name, nor did I know any famous Keys throughout history, but something told me he came from a powerful family. He had the education, dressed like he had money, and I'd never been around someone whose magic was quite that strong before.

I was glad I kissed him. I'd hate to rip off the bisexual Band-aid with someone and find out they were a bigot.

There was a knock on the door, and Gabriel rushed in with his umbrella. It was storming pretty badly outside.

"Did you know there's a werewolf with a big lump on his head passed the fuck out on the grass?"

Ravyn just shrugged.

"He cheated on me and then had the nerve to get mad Killian and Key are staying with me. He had it coming."

"What did you hit him with, a two by four? He's totally soaked but still out."

"With my fist," Key grunted. "You'd do the same if someone was treating your librarian the way Valentine has been treating Ravyn."

"Oh, that's Valentine? Ripley hates him and told us what he did. Good job, my man," Gabriel said, holding up his fist.

I'd go check on him, even after what he did to Ravyn if he weren't intent on using my girlfriend to raise a deranged cult. I could even overlook being dumb enough to think he hadn't done anything wrong if he were hurt. But, putting my witch in danger like that?

Fuck him.

I didn't know Gabriel as well as I knew Felix, but he was family now. And he wasn't family you tried to avoid at functions either. Gabriel was cool. I didn't know why his familiar was still a snake, but that was between the two of them.

"So, we need to call the four elements to open the puzzle box found at the ruins where the cult died," Ravyn said.

"Need? Do we really *need* to open a box from the Cult of the Aether Sisters?" Gabriel said.

"Does my sister *need* feral books that bite? You have that look in your eyes of a man that's been assaulted by one of her books before."

"One of them ruined my favorite shirt."

"So, her thing is books, and this is mine. Key is an expert on the cult, and relics are my specialty. The cult didn't make this box. It's too advanced. We have this theory that since they weren't witches, they wouldn't have been able to call the elements to open it."

Gabriel ran his finger over the copper puzzle box.

"Ripley told me you think Valentine is under the influence of the cult. How do you know someone didn't come along later and plant this who also got whispered to?"

That was also a theory, but I doubted it. Necromancy didn't need an eclipse. If someone had gone to the site with that intent, the spirits would have killed them because the time wasn't right. They didn't want to be noticed or raised until this eclipse.

"No one knew about the underground chamber until Valentine was able to get close enough to the ruins," Key said. "This site isn't like other haunted sites humans flock to for entertainment. The locals don't advertise and try to cash in on the ghosts like many places. The only reason they let Valentine do an excavation there was that he signed a contract in blood promising the rites would be done and they'd be rid of the ghosts."

"How did *were* the rites done?" Gabriel asked. "Lilith said they weren't witches."

"I drink, and I know things," Key said.

"Dude, you are the only person I've met that is as tall as a god. You can't quote Tyrion Lannister with no context," Gabriel said.

Key just shrugged.

"The Cult of the Aether Sisters were hybrids. Bastardizations of shifters and witches, but not the same because the god that created them was different. You would literally never need the knowledge to do the rites for them because it's already been done. Can we focus on the box?"

"Yeah, sure, but if anything crazy pops out, you tell your sister I had my reservations about doing this."

"Nothing is going to pop out," I said. "This is just the first puzzle. They'll get more complicated the more we unlock."

"Shall we pick elements?" Ravyn said.

Here went nothing.

CHAPTER 28

Ravyn

I knew Gabriel didn't get a scholarship to a magical academy, even though he should have. People were dicks. I didn't know Key's first name, much less where he went to school, and that should have bothered me, considering he was sleeping in my bed, but it didn't. Still, I knew every person in this warehouse was proficient at calling the elements.

No one was going to blow shit up, calling fire, or cause a thunderstorm in here like what was going on outside. Some of my classmates did that at the academy. Our Elemental Magic professor had patience in spades because some people did it more than once.

"I get fire," Key said.

Everyone wanted fire. It was badass and the hardest to master. Only seniors were allowed to play with the elements in their dorm rooms. If you needed to light candles or incense and you weren't old enough, you had to use a lighter like a human. Way too many freshmen nearly burned the dorms down trying.

Everyone thought fire was the best, but I liked air too. It

153

was also difficult to control. You could call a gentle breeze and blow out your candles, or you could uproot an entire tree. I claimed wind.

Gabriel played well on my sister's team, and he was a good fit here too. He didn't argue with anyone about an element or brag about his skills. Killian took earth, and Gabriel grabbed water.

I was *dying* to know what would be revealed with the first puzzle, but my phone rang, and it was my twin. She didn't keep her men on leashes, and she never called during work hours. We texted all the time, but phone calls never happened unless it was an emergency. Unfortunately, my twin sister had been having a lot of those lately.

"It's Ripley. I have to get this."

"She'd better be okay," Gabriel growled.

If she was calling me and not him, it wasn't a library emergency, but something was up. I went to one of the side rooms for privacy,

"What's up?"

"Girl, I fucked up. I think I'm in trouble."

"Tell me what you did, and we'll figure out how to make it go away. Reyson is probably better at making corpses go away than I am, though."

"I don't think there's a way out of this. So, Reyson let it slip he sees babies in the possibilities for my future. I was thinking pretty far in the future. We had *a lot* of sex to celebrate the victory in Hell. Like, many orgies, and we broke out all my good toys. Bram did this thing with his tongue piercing that—"

"Focus. I fail to see how Bram's piercing and orgies equate emergency."

"You *know* I'm meticulous about birth control spells. Reyson had to do something extra because he's more potent than my magic. I don't know anything about God birth control and how often it needs to be redone. I *do,* however, know that I was kidnapped and in a cage in Hell when I was supposed to be redoing mine. Then the whole revolution thing happened. A stupid kid messed up my library while I was gone, and when I was finally back in my apartment with all of them together, I was thinking about orgies and not birth control with everything that happened. What if I'm pregnant?"

"You always said you wanted kids, eventually. Your guys are insane, but I'll bet they'll make amazing daddies."

"Yeah, *eventually.* After I met the right guy, had lots of sex, and traveled."

"You met five Mister Rights and traveled to a different realm. You don't even know if you're pregnant, and it's too soon to test."

"I have a feeling, and you know how things go when I get those."

Yeah, things tended to get fucked when either of us caught a feeling. I was in the exact same situation because I caught feelings for Killian and Key. I just knew damned sure I did my birth control spell before I got kinky with them.

"Shit, you're definitely pregnant then. Congrats. After we open this box, I'll boot Gabriel back to the library so you can tell them."

"How am I supposed to tell them that? Yeah, we're all copacetic and living together, but we haven't even been dating a year."

"Girl, seriously? They went to Hell for you. Impregnating you is just the next step."

"Gross, Ravyn."

"That was nowhere near as nasty as when Mom tried to tell us how babies are made."

"I thought we swore never to discuss that again."

"Hey, I didn't bring up the drawings she did."

"What if the baby is Reyson's? What if giving birth to a demigod is like those Sigourney Weaver movies where those things punch their way out of your chest?"

I was fairly certain that was unlikely, but we couldn't exactly find a YouTube video for that. I'd be looking up something totally harmless, and it would autocomplete some really bizarre question about pregnancy, but nothing about demigods.

"Reyson tends to spill his guts about things no one wants to know about. He'd tell you if his spawn was going to eat its way out of you. Plus, he'd probably murder someone for messing up your hair. He wouldn't say he wanted kids with you if it would kill you."

"Shit. You're right. I'm going to tell them over dinner. I don't want them making a scene at the library if I'm wrong. Most of my regulars are grandparents. This baby is going to have so many booties and knitted caps."

"You still have to confirm you're pregnant."

"It was the right time and *a lot* of dicks."

"Congrats. I'll get your man back to you unharmed."

"If he gets cursed opening your new toy, I expect him back uncursed."

"He'll be totally fine."

We were finally ready to open that box. I was about ninety-eight percent sure I wasn't going to get my sister's boyfriend cursed and way less sure I wasn't going to make a total dick out of myself trying to keep my sister's secret.

R ipley's news wasn't mine to tell, and I would *never* betray my twin. Especially over something this important. I knew she was terrified now, but once it sunk in, she was going to be ecstatic if it was true. We both loved kids and wanted them. They were like these pint-sized terrorists that said whatever they were feeling and fuck your feelings. Only kids and senior citizens could get away with that. It was pretty amazing.

"Is Ripley okay?" Gabriel asked.

"Girl talk, and I had to swear I wasn't going to send you back as a plague-ridden rat."

"That's not a good pep talk if you want my help."

"Cheer up, sparky. No one has turned into a rodent since I started working here," I said, smacking him on the back.

"I trust *you*. I don't trust the Cult of the Aether Sisters."

"This is a relatively common puzzle when it comes to these things," Killian said.

"Well, let's get it done then."

The puzzle box was on a stand with all sides available to hit with magic. I'd seen Key break out Old Norse and all this knowledge, but I'd never actually seen him do magic since he got here. Key must have done *something* to get Valentine to be his little bitch.

Key had this twisted sense of humor I just adored. We held our breath as we called the elements towards our rune. Key didn't look worried at all and aimed his fire with finger guns. It was fucked up, and I loved it.

The gears on the box started moving, and this was *definitely* not made by the cult. It was too advanced. The top of the box sprung, and no stinky black smoke came out to curse us. Score one for the home team.

The sides of the puzzle box collapsed to reveal a slightly smaller box and the new puzzle. Unfortunately, there weren't any runes etched into the box this time.

Fuck me sideways. This box had an ancient fingerprint scanner.

CHAPTER 30

Ravyn

What the actual fuck was I looking at? There was a glowing blue thumbprint on the side of the box. Since I got hired, we'd received several puzzle boxes at the museum, and my parents used to get me one for our birthday. But I'd *never* seen one like this before.

"What the shit?" Killian said. "This technology wasn't around then. So we're fucked because we don't even know whose thumbprint it wants."

"I was going to stay and watch, but I guess this is it?" Gabriel said. "Sorry, guys. I know you wanted to get inside this box."

I gave Gabriel a big hug. I knew my sister's boyfriends well enough to know they were going to be ecstatic at the possibility of little Ripleys running around the library. I was too. I needed to get some yarn so I could start knitting. I didn't even know for sure, but I trusted my twin's gut.

"Get back home to my sister."

"You said she was okay?"

"She'll be just fine. How have things been for you since Kaine's press conference?"

Gabriel smirked.

"Kaine let it slip that I knew how to kill a revenant with magic. The same people who wouldn't piss on me if I were on fire have called me with job offers. The Academy of the Profane didn't give me a scholarship or allow me into their school and let me work to pay for my tuition, but they called and offered me a teaching job."

I squealed and hugged him again.

"If you take it, that means our family is dominating the Profane triquetra. It's an enormous honor to be invited to teach there. It's much bigger than getting a scholarship. They don't post teaching jobs, even if someone is retiring and they have an opening. Unlike some of the spots they give to the students, they don't care about your ancestors or money. They are after your skill set. Minerva Krauss doesn't have some famous family line or come from money, but they begged her to teach there for years before she finally gave in."

"That's the only offer I'm seriously considering," Gabriel said.

"I'm so proud," Killian said, punching him in the arm.

"Thanks. Now, I *suspect* something is going on with my girlfriend, so I need to go."

We watched Gabriel go. I knew that wasn't a conversation I needed to be a part of, but I'd *love* to be a fly on the wall when that group found out my sister's news. Reyson lost his shit over random shit we took for granted in this century. I brought him a box of Twinkies for shits and giggles, and you would have thought they were pure gold based on his reaction. His face when he found out he might be a daddy? Yeah, I wanted to watch that.

I needed a pick me up because we were fucked as far as opening this puzzle box went. Minerva was a genius figuring out how to pick a blood lock without dying, but that just involved overwhelming the lock with blood and not pricking your finger on it. Tricking a fingerprint scanner, even one this old? I doubted she had figured that out. But I had an idea. My sister had a whole harem with skills.

"If *anyone* knows how to get around a fingerprint scanner, it's going to be Balthazar," I said, grabbing my phone.

"He's good, but can he hack a puzzle box? This thing doesn't exactly have an internet connection," Killian said.

"You don't need to bother your sister's boyfriend," Key said. "I know how to open it."

"How in actual fuck—"

"Just watch. Do you trust me?"

"Well, yeah. You wouldn't be sleeping in my bed if I didn't."

"Remember that after all this. That was all the real me."

Key looked horribly sorry for something, like I would be furious at him when he opened that box. I was expecting a big show of magic. There was basically none of that. He pressed his thumb on the box, and there was this explosion of light that knocked me on my ass.

What in actual fuck was happening right now, and how did his thumbprint unlock that box? I tried to shake the black spots from my vision as Killian helped me to my feet.

There were two men in my museum dressed and painted like Vikings that weren't here before. One of them was tall and fierce with blond hair and ice blue eyes. He was definitely supernatural, but I couldn't tell what he was. He fell to his feet and started *groveling* before Key.

I couldn't tell what the other man was either. He had long brown hair with patches of white in it. It was unusual, and I knew they didn't have a good developer bleach back then, so it was natural. This dude flung himself at Key, and the two embraced like they were old friends.

"Key? I think it's time to tell us your first name," I said.

He was still hugging the man who popped out of the puzzle box and just looked so excited he was out.

"Lo."

"Lo? Your name *is not* Lo Key. Stop fucking with us."

Key slightly bowed his head. When his gaze met mine again, his eyes were silver like Lilith and Reyson's, and his aura was just as golden as the two gods I'd met so far. Lo Key?

"Oh, shit. You're Loki," I whispered.

CHAPTER 31

Loki

I had been dreading this moment, but it needed to happen this way. I needed Valentine and all his people to think I was a warlock because if the Cult of the Aether Sisters knew Loki had contacted him, the only way I would get on that dig to get rid of their spirits and fetch my box would be through violence.

I *was not* a violent god. I found it senseless and pointless. Especially when a little trickery and some lies could easily get you what you wanted. The spirits of the Cult of the Aether sister didn't go quietly. They would have recognized my face, but my aura and eyes confused them since I shape shifted into a warlock. They fought, but in the end, I won. This prophecy was another story.

I didn't *want* to deceive Ravyn or Killian. I wasn't expecting to like them so much. I'd been alive a long time and honestly didn't like most people. But those two? They were keepers.

I definitely should have told them before I revealed my secret weapons. I just didn't know how after a time. I guess I thought it was kind of like ripping duct tape off someone's mouth. Best to just do it and hope they don't start screaming.

"Why did you lie?" Ravyn said. "Are you here to make sure the cult comes back? Who are these people?"

"The only thing I ever fibbed about was my name and being a warlock. Everything else was really me. I'm here to make damned sure that prophesy never comes true. I made this box when I heard about the prophecy. The Cult of the Aether Sisters stole it and had been trying to figure out how to open it, but I made it impossible. This is Bjorn and Sleipnir."

"Wasn't Sleipnir—"

"My son," I said. "He can shift into an eight-legged horse, but he prefers spending his time as a man. Stupid Odin stole him from me and forced him to stay as a horse because he's powerful. I stole him back as soon as I could and placed him in this box with Bjorn so Odin would leave him alone. Odin and I have made our peace, and he's not looking for my son anymore."

"When you said you once went to great lengths to stop an arranged marriage, you meant when you shape shifted into a mare in heat and distracted the stallion doing the work on the fortification of Asgard, so Freya didn't have to marry that giant. And then you ended up giving birth to an eight legged horse."

"When they teach that story, do they also tell you that they blamed me for the collective decision to sell Freya, the sun, and the moon, which they didn't own, by the way, to the giant if he could complete the job in the agreed upon time?"

"But why did you lie to us, and how does this all tie into the cult?"

I needed to take care of Bjorn and Sleipnir. They both agreed to go in the box for different reasons. I sent them to a pocket realm with all kinds of comforts and food. Unfortunately, they weren't exactly dressed for this century, and they didn't understand a word of that conversation.

I waved my hand and dressed them both in modern clothes. I gave them the ability to understand all languages.

"This is the witch with the black lips I saw in my vision," Bjorn said.

"Is Odin still looking for me?" Sleipnir asked.

"All my contemporaries have either fucked off to the Aether or trying to hold down mundane jobs. Odin is off in Paris writing books."

"I *like* you, Loki, and I'm hoping you have a very good explanation for all of this. Why don't we go home, and you can explain over some takeout? My cottage has extra rooms. They can stay in my guest rooms if I like what you have to say. If I don't, the three of you can fuck off my property."

I was grateful she was willing to hear me out because something told me this witch didn't suffer fools that betrayed her. The only reason Valentine wasn't cursed seven ways to Sunday was that she valued her job. I had a feeling it was coming.

I had an excellent reason for deceiving everyone here at the museum and could explain that. Hopefully, she accepted my reasons for the other shit, too, because I was the god responsible for creating the Cult of the Aether Sisters.

CHAPTER 32

Karyn

I tried not to be mad Loki lied to us, but I let this man in my bed. He knew my sister was dating a god and that I'd met Lilith, and he still didn't tell us. Honestly, Doctor Key really being Loki in disguise made a lot of fucking sense if I thought about it, but what was his interest in the Cult of the Aether Sisters?

Loki had helped his fellow gods plenty of times, but he also shit on them quite often. Sometimes, they had it coming, and sometimes they didn't. Though, if Odin kidnapped his son and forced him to be a horse, I could see where some of the stories I had been told might be a little biased against Loki. I'd never once been told or read anything about the Norse gods that Sleipnir was a horse shifter and frankly hot as fuck when he was human.

We were walking back to my cottage. Bjorn didn't talk much and seemed to just be taking everything in. What was he anyway? I still couldn't tell. Sleipnir and Loki were adorable with their reunion. They were just as close as I was with my mom. From what I remembered, Loki had shape shifted into many different things and was both a mother and a father to many creatures.

Killian caught up with me. He had to be feeling what I was feeling. He went bisexual for Loki. We'd both fooled around with him.

"Why do you think Loki is at your museum? Why lie about the puzzle box if he made it and had people stashed inside?"

"No idea. He's always felt right with us, though. Even though he's shifted his aura and eyes back to a god instead of a warlock, he still feels like one of us. Can't you feel it?"

"It's weird, but I do. You know how I feel about lying, though."

"Unless he can god mojo all four elements at once, he needed four witches to get to that thumbprint."

"So, why didn't he just lead with he's fucking Loki, had some people inside, and had us call Gabriel? Gabriel has seen Reyson naked. He's not going to care about another god. Unless Reyson and Loki know each other and Reyson would tell us not to help him."

We hadn't realized they had caught up with us as I was unlocking the door.

"Reyson, as he's calling himself now, and I go way back. We bonded over being gods people like to shit on. When they locked me in a cave and tortured me with snake venom, they intended to just leave me there. All their followers thought I would be there until Ragnarok. Reyson sprung me. We hung out for a while, then parted ways. The two of us together tended to attract angry villagers with pitchforks. Now that you know the truth, I'd love to brunch with him and catch up."

That was fucked up. My life was fucked up. Damn Reyson and his possibilities. That fucker probably *knew* Loki was at my museum and didn't tell my twin. She *defi-*

nitely would have told me. Loki probably had some long-winded explanation for lying to me that I might not like. Reyson stuck his god dick in my twin sister and had been around her long enough to know the twin bond was sacred. If he wasn't keeping secrets from Ripley, then he definitely needed to tell me there was a trickster god pretending to be a warlock giving me epic cunnilingus and making out with my familiar.

I think I was more pissed at Reyson than I was Loki, and I knew that wasn't rational.

"What are we ordering?" I asked as we moved into my living room. "What do your people eat?"

"That's a complicated question, Ravyn. I put them in a pocket realm with plenty of resources, but all they know is what they ate back in their time."

"A side of beef is delicious in any century," Sleipnir said.

"I've gotten many visions of the future," Bjorn said. "I saw one where they stick beef between strange bread with vegetables."

"I remember you telling me about that. It sounds like a good way to ruin beef. It's best roasted over a spit or served in a stew," Sleipnir said.

Oh, I was going to have fun corrupting this bunch if I didn't end up booting them out of my house. And that answered at least one question about Bjorn. He was a seer. One who could have given the Cult of the Aether Sisters their prophesies about the eclipse and started this nonsense.

"Okay, so it's my solemn duty as a geriatric millennial to corrupt you with Kobe cheeseburgers, duck fat and truffle frites, and some panko-crusted onion rings."

"That sounds amazing," Killian moaned.

"I don't know what any of that is," Sleipnir said.

"I told you when we agreed to go in the box that a black lipped witch would be our guide when we entered the world again. This is the witch from my vision. We should eat it," Bjorn said.

What the actual fuck? Loki already had his phone out ordering. Why was his seer looking to me instead of him? He was a god, and I didn't actually have any idea what was going on.

Killian and I sat on my love seat across from Loki and his crew on my couch. Sleipnir and Loki had different hair, but they shared a good bit of their facial features, and Sleipnir was probably bigger than his...mom? What was the term for that?

"Ravyn and Killian, I'm sorry I didn't tell you who I really was. I wanted to. I *should* have. Valentine was the only one I needed to think I was a warlock after a time. It's not that I don't trust you. At first, I thought you would react badly because of the stories told about me. After a while, I knew you wouldn't. I guess I didn't because it was just so nice being myself without all the god bullshit. I could be myself without the expectations of being all powerful and the horse shit that is now associated with Loki. Some of those movies aren't even remotely accurate."

That made sense, I guess. Reyson reveled in being a god, but Lilith didn't. She stepped away and retired until she couldn't anymore. Loki was kind of a strange friot. There were people who thought he was wholly evil, people like me and Killian who found him a little ambiguous, and people who still worshipped him because they thrived on chaos. I could see where he wouldn't have known where we stood.

"We're listening, and I haven't cursed that beautiful cock of yours yet. So set the record straight," I said.

"For both of us," Killian said.

"Wait a minute," I said, thinking back to my history classes. "Isn't your happy god ass *married*? Maybe you should have led with that before you kissed both of us."

Sleipnir shot Loki this look like he was used to him doing

shit like this. Loki *knew* how I felt about cheating. I wasn't just against getting cheated on. I wasn't going to do that to another person either. Booting him out of my life was seeming like a good idea.

"I *was* married. A very long time ago. She tried to take care of me when they bound me in a cave a tortured me with snake venom, but they murdered our sons right in front of us. They used the entrails of one to bind me. When I was free, she blamed everything on me and left. I ran into her in the sixteenth century. She has a bit of a vampire fetish now."

"Didn't all that start because you killed Odin's son Baldur?" Killian asked.

Loki just shrugged.

"Yeah, I arranged for his son to be killed. One of his sons. Do you know how many of mine those assholes went after?"

"So, tell us the real story," Killian said.

"I fathered three children with Angrboda. Fenrir could shift into a powerful wolf. Werewolves were already a thing, but they still feared him. His brother, Jormungand, could turn into a serpent, and another god had already created the basilisks. Hel wasn't dual natured, but her appearance gave them pause. Half of her was beautiful, and the other half resembled a corpse. Still, she was mine, and I loved her. They *stole* them from me, and now all three of them are in the Aether."

"Isn't Hel the Goddess of Death?" Killian asked.

"That's just the horse shit they *want* you to think. There is only one Death, though he goes by many different names throughout history and different cultures. He's pretty cool, and the bastard owes me two hundred dollars. They tortured all three of them to see how powerful they were, then murdered them. Sleipnir wasn't killed, but they forced him to be Odin's pet. All of my children were just as precious as

Baldur was to Odin and Frigg. They should have thought about the parental bond before they came for mine."

That made sense. Reyson would have razed the entire cosmos if someone came after just one person he loved. He hadn't even met Lilith when he was plotting to do damage to the god who bullied her. Hell, that wasn't even a god thing. When I was a kid, one of the kindergarten moms threatened to yeet a five-year-old for being mean to her child.

"Okay, so I get your motivations there. How does that tie into the Cult of the Aether Sisters and the box that ended up at my museum?"

"Bjorn and the bear mages were my creations. As you can see, Bjorn is perfectly sane. At first, the bear mages were part of my family, but things quickly changed. They went insane and fucked off to form a cult."

Okay, we'd gotten this far, and I really wanted one of those cheeseburgers. Unfortunately, the delivery person wasn't here yet.

"So, why in the actual fuck did you make bear witches, and where were you when they started killing people? And how did that end with Bjorn and your son in a box?" I asked.

I really hoped he had a suitable answer for that.

I really hoped Loki had a decent explanation for all this because I had this nasty feeling in the pit of my gut that all that kissing and those feelings I was having were just him taking the piss. Had one of history's most famous tricksters tricked me? Did he suggest spin the bottle just to fuck with me?

We all saw how Lilith was with her creations. She only wanted to kill them in extreme circumstances, and some of them were dumb enough to attack her. Was Loki like that with his?

"I need to go back to the killing of Baldur. I didn't do it directly. I tricked someone else into doing it. Those stupid bastards blamed everything on me, but they were actually right that time. They honestly made it easy.

"I could have gone after any of their sons to make my point that I was angry about them messing with my kids, but Baldur was this golden boy. Every god has some form of foresight. He started having dreams of his death. So his mother, Frigg, went around securing oaths from everyone that he wouldn't be harmed.

173

"The other gods were so sure nothing was going to happen to him. So they would amuse themselves by throwing weapons at him. It was pretty fucked up. I mean, if you love your kid, you just do not throw sharp things at them or let other people do that."

I could agree with him on that one. If your son was having visions of his own death, inviting people to throw shit at him was just tempting fate. Gods weren't immune to fate shite either. Reyson sure got dragged into it.

"Anyway, none of those weapons would have killed him. They just bounced off of him. Mistletoe was the only weapon that would kill Baldur. I made a spear with it and gave it to Hodr, who was blind as fuck. Baldur just stood there like a dumbass while Hodr threw it at him and ended up dead. They got *really* angry with me, even though they knew that shit was coming and made it easy by throwing weapons at him over brunch."

None of us were angry he killed Baldur. He didn't sound the least bit sorry about it, but technically they came for his offspring first. I still didn't know what this story had to do with him making bear witches and a seer.

"Odin was my blood brother. I thought of the rest of them like family, even as they blamed me for all their shit decisions and generally shat all over me when I stepped in and fixed their problems. It became crystal clear I needed to make a point, and I did. They didn't think about my three children they tortured and killed. They didn't think about Sleipnir being kept in Odin's stable with a magical collar that forced him to be a horse. To them, I had committed the ultimate crime."

"While this is fascinating, and they sound like utter fuck heads, what does that have to do with where we are now?" Ravyn said.

Loki sighed.

"I don't get close to people very often. I never know if they like me or the whole Loki mythology god thing. I need you and Killian to know the full story with nothing left out because I know I fucked up keeping the whole god thing a secret and not sharing everything I knew. I enjoy your company, and I want to keep enjoying it. So, I need you to know everything."

So did I, and it meant a lot to me that he hadn't been fucking with either of us this entire time. Ravyn was only just starting to trust men again. It would have destroyed her, and yeah, frankly, it would have hurt my fucking feelings too.

"Go on."

"Okay, so I fucked off away from them, but I always intended to get Sleipnir back. They relentlessly hunted me everywhere. I decided to make a new family. I had my wife and sons with me. We built a remote cabin that would be hard for Odin to find. I created Bjorn and the hybrids.

"We were a family at first, and the cult didn't *use* to be bad. Bjorn could see if Odin or anyone else was zeroing in on us so we could move. A good bit of the spells at the beginning of that grimoire, I wrote with them together. They were *supposed* to be good.

"We came up with a plan to rescue Sleipnir. Bjorn was able to tell us the perfect time to strike. They were holding a feast in Odin's Hall. I wasn't invited, of course, but they had weird rules about table manners. They were actively hunting me and hated everything I stood for, but if I claimed the rules of hospitality, they had to feed me and not do anything to me.

"It was their stupid rule, and I was going to twist it to my benefit. So I sat there insulting them to their faces. I hurled all their fuckups at them without telling them what they did to me because I needed to keep my cool. Of course, they tried to get under my skin, but when you think you're the best thing since herbed goat cheese, it's pretty easy to insult you."

"They got me out," Sleipnir said. "While my mother was insulting them, the hybrids snuck into my stable. Some of them were gifted blacksmiths. They could get my collar off. I shifted back, and they had clothes waiting. We snuck out, and one of them put a signal into the sky to Loki. He met us outside, and we left. It seriously pissed the other gods off when they realized I was missing."

I cocked my eyebrow at Sleipnir.

"You don't talk like an ancient Viking."

"Oh, I upgraded both of them," Loki said. "They understand all modern language and slang. I *hate* it when people don't get my memes, and it will help them fit in."

"So, you got Sleipnir out. How did your bear witches turn into a cult?" Ravyn asked.

All three men sighed.

"Angrboda," they all said.

"Wasn't she the mother of your children that were slain?" I asked.

"Not the same woman," Loki said, running his fingers through his hair. "Her name was Thorunn, but she decided to call herself Angrboda after the mother of some of my children. It pissed my wife off to no end. She wasn't a god, but she wanted to be. I made her powerful. They all were, but it wasn't enough for her."

"She hated me," Sleipnir said. "She hated Loki paid attention to me, and she didn't think they should have rescued me. The gods started hunting my mother even harder after they stole me back. Our family had to move often. I'm not going to call her Angrboda. I never did. Her name was Thorunn. Thorunn started whispering to the others that they could have everything if it weren't for me. She elevated herself to a god."

"She was doing this in secret," Bjorn said. "None of us knew, but I had a vision. Thorunn had everyone on her side. She had convinced them she was a god, and they intended to run. It was a two-part vision. First, Loki was going to be caught by the gods that day. His creations were going to betray him. He could do nothing to stop them *then*, but others would. He would be in the right position to stop them at the next eclipse in the future."

"If I hadn't done things exactly as I had done back then, Bjorn and Sleipnir would have died," Loki said. "The hybrids were plotting, and so were we. Bjorn tried to nip it in the bud by telling them they would meet a horrible end if they went the route they were planning. Thorunn tortured him until he revealed they could possibly return the next time the moon totally disappeared.

"Sleipnir burst in and rescued Bjorn. The hybrids were good, but they aren't as fast as an eight-legged horse. I had just enough time to make the box with the pocket dimension and get Bjorn and Sleipnir inside before the other gods descended on me.

"I turned into a salmon and hid in a nearby stream, but I left a net so that they would know where I was. I needed them looking for me because I knew the hybrids would go back to my cabin to rob me. They'd want Bjorn for his seer abilities, and they'd want to sacrifice Sleipnir if they didn't turn him back over to Odin.

"I let myself get caught, and when they searched my cabin, they found my box and none of the people they were looking for. I know you've heard stories about what they did. Imagine how many followers they would have gathered and the carnage they could have wrought with a seer. But Bjorn is my creation, and I wouldn't leave him to that fate.

"I knew I wasn't going to be in that cave forever. I networked with other gods. I knew some of them would hear about what happened and think I deserved to rot. I also knew there were several that knew how upset I was about my children and thought I was perfectly justified in my revenge. It was Chaos who eventually came and broke my chains."

"Wait, Reyson knew about the Cult of the Aether Sisters this entire time?" I demanded.

What the actual shit? The man went into long ass soliloquies any time he knew something we didn't or if he just wanted to talk about modern junk food. He *knew* Ravyn was getting these items. He was there when Lilith said the cult wasn't her creation, and she didn't know who made them.

"I'm pretty sure he didn't," Loki said. "They didn't call themselves the Cult of the Aether Sisters. They didn't call themselves anything at all. A historian gave them that name hundreds of years later, and it stuck. By the time Reyson came for me, I had heard they were dead. I was still bitter about the entire thing. We didn't talk much about the hybrids. He knew I found my son and lost him to keep him safe. Reyson knew I tried my hand at creations, and it went horribly wrong except for Bjorn, who I also had to send away, but he didn't know the details of the hybrids."

We still had a *lot* more to talk about, but the doorbell rang because our food was here. Ravyn jumped up to get the door. I was pretty sure food delivery wasn't a concept back then or even in the pocket dimension he was in, but Sleipnir jumped up to help her.

I got what Loki had told us, and it sounded like he had shit choices no matter what he did. Though I would have imagined if you wanted to get revenge on your blood brother for hurting your kids, he could have guessed how Odin and the rest of his god friends were going to react to killing Baldur.

He didn't create the hybrids to be what they became. They betrayed him. But I still thought we were missing a good bit of history about his creations, and we weren't going to bed until he spilled.

CHAPTER 34

Sleipnir

I could understand everything that was being said now, but not quite everything that was going on. We were meant to be eating, but there were no farm animals or crops on this property. My mother could conjure food, but he didn't do that this time. So I followed the witch out of the hearth because she said the food was here. How? No one cooked anything.

Ravyn opened the door, and a young vampire handed her a bunch of bags that frankly smelled amazing. Maybe they didn't totally ruin the beef with this whole cheeseburger nonsense. Ravyn turned around and ran straight into my chest.

She smelled amazing, and she was quite pretty. Bjorn had seen her in a vision and told me she would be a vital part of our lives. Bjorn was *never* wrong; it was just he didn't always get the full picture. Like the fact that she was clearly into my mom, and things had gone down with them while we were in the pocket dimension.

Bjorn and I just had each other in that pocket dimension.

There wasn't a single pretty woman in sight. I wouldn't mind showing Ravyn my longsword in action, but I wouldn't do that to my mom.

We just sort of stood there smashed together for a minute before she cleared her throat and took a step back.

"Did you pay that vampire to hunt for us?"

"What? No. He picked up our food from the restaurant that prepared it. I paid the restaurant for the food, a delivery fee to go towards his salary, and I gave him a big tip."

"Sounds like extortion."

"It's a fee for the convenience. You're going to love this cheeseburger, by the way."

"Hey, please don't get too mad at my mom for lying to you about being Loki. You don't know what it was like back then. He's not a violent person. He gets things done another way. Brute strength was what was respected. Odin did all this shit to gain knowledge, and everyone respected him for it. Loki is cunning, and everyone shit on him for it. They thought since he didn't solve things with a weapon or sacrifice something for the way his brain worked, he was dangerous."

"I'm not mad at him for being Loki. Killian and I aren't people who think he's inherently evil. We're upset about the secrets. He should have told *both* of us before he kissed us. Killian has been in my life for a long time, and I love him. I could get over him lying to me but not hurting Killian."

Oh. Oh! It was like that. I was never really around Lilith's witches much. They were hardcore into Lilith and never paid the other gods much attention like the humans and some of the other supernatural races at the time.

I was stolen from Loki as soon as I was born after Odin realized I had eight legs when I was a horse and could travel between realms. He put a collar on me that trapped me as a horse and stuck me in his stables. There weren't any witches around when I was growing up. After Loki freed me, I was around his hybrids for a short time before I had to go to the pocket realm for my safety.

I knew how my mother felt about his lovers. The only reason he didn't have more than one when I was freed was that he promised his wife he wouldn't. This witch took lovers like my mother, and that was fascinating.

"So, you and Killian are together, and you, Killian, and my mother are together? Is that common in this century?"

"You're adorable in this big, sexy beefcake way. It's common with witches. Have you not met one before, big guy?"

"Actually, no. I was a horse for a long time, and then I had to go in the pocket dimension. Bjorn hasn't either, but he's seen them in visions. Clearly, not everything."

"Oh, I'm going to have so much fun corrupting the two of you," she purred.

Was she hitting on me? What would my mother say about that? Was this a witch thing?

"Ravyn, you can hit on my son any time. We're all hungry, and I still have more to tell you," Loki called from the kitchen.

He knew, and he wasn't upset with me? All the gods I knew tended to be the jealous sort.

"That's our cue. And you're going to be fully converted to cheeseburgers after you eat this."

"Bjorn says he saw you in a vision and that you would help us stop Thorunn from returning. He kept saying we would have a witch guide. I don't think that was in matters of ruining a good cow."

"Come on, big guy. You'll be thanking me when you cum in your pants after you've taken a bite."

"I only do that when it's appropriate."

"We're not at the point in our relationship to talk about

your dick just yet, but I'm curious about what they say about horses. Come on."

This witch was quite forward. I could see why my mother was smitten and kept being Loki a secret until he absolutely had to reveal the truth. I just hoped Ravyn and Killian understood that because Loki deserved to be happy.

I couldn't control my visions or what I saw. They just happened, and sometimes I saw terrible things. But, I didn't regret the gift Loki gave me when he created me because I saw wonderful things too. I helped Loki save his child, and we would stop Thorunn from returning.

Sleipnir and I were the only people in the pocket realm. He was a lot more restless than I was because he was a prisoner once before. When he was shifted, he could run to any realm he liked. He could have run straight out of the realm we were in back home, but he trusted his mother.

After being trapped as a horse and barely spoken to, Sleipnir craved human contact. I tried to keep him entertained, and we were close friends, but I think he would have been happier if more people were there with us.

We were there a long time. I didn't have my vision of Ravyn until we were already there, but I saw her more than once. I told Sleipnir about all of my visions, but it was different for him because he didn't see them like I did. I didn't see Loki in a relationship with Ravyn and Killian, but it didn't really surprise me.

I didn't quite understand the vision of a place with yellow arches outside that served beef between strange bread, but it seemed popular. Honestly, I still didn't understand why I saw that, but I trusted Ravyn and Loki with the cheeseburgers a lot more than Sleipnir did.

Killian and Loki had already started devouring theirs. Ravyn was watching us with this naughty look on her face. It was kind of sexy. The cheeseburgers smelled amazing, and I wanted to try it, but we needed to get Sleipnir on board, or he would sneak out and try to kill something to eat. Loki looked wholly amused and that he knew the same thing I did.

"Son, the rules of hospitality are much different in this century, but it's generally considered rude to turn your nose up at something you haven't tried because you don't think you'll like it."

"That doesn't look like any bread I've eaten before."

"Will you please just take a bite and try it? You can spit it out if you don't like it, and I'll order you something else."

"Weird déjà vu," Ravyn said. "My mom used to say something similar to Ripley and me all the time if she cooked a new recipe. We always like it. Take a big bite for me, big guy."

Sleipnir looked so confused. I'd been around him enough to know he loved the attention of a pretty woman but would have feelings about getting them from one involved with his mother. Loki seemed to have no issue with it at all and just gave Sleipnir an encouraging nod.

Sleipnir finally picked up his cheeseburger so that I could eat mine. I took a bite and groaned as a combination of the juices from the meat, bread, and cheese hit my mouth. If Sleipnir didn't like this, I might have to revoke his friend card after all our centuries together.

"Oh, wow. I didn't mess my pants up, but that's superb," Sleipnir groaned.

What exactly had Ravyn said to him when they disappeared? I didn't have super hearing like Loki did, but I could guess. This witch was totally inappropriate, and I loved it.

"Now that Sleipnir and Bjorn have tried a new food and we are getting to eat, there's still more you need to know about the cult."

"Yes, we do need to know more about them," Killian said.

"Okay, so the last time I talked to Reyson, he didn't have any creations, and I haven't met any since then, so he might not have explained this. Lilith had way too much going on when you met her. We can create a vessel and give it magical powers, but intelligence and personality are something we don't dictate.

"Thorunn wasn't the smartest hybrid I made. Most of the spells in the grimoire were written by Asfrid and I. Asfrid was brilliant, but a little meek. Thorunn wasn't even the strongest at magic or when she was shifted. She did have a ton of charisma and a fat head."

She really did. She took the whole Angrboda thing way too far because she was obsessed with Loki. Loki viewed all of us like his children. He was never interested in having sex with us, and he promised his wife not to. Much of what he would say next was news to me, too, because I didn't know what happened after they captured him.

"After Reyson freed me, I shape shifted into a warlock like you see now. It kept people off my trail. I went around asking about them. Thorunn went around trying to convince everyone she was Angrboda. She traveled to different villages and tried to perform magic tricks or shift into a bear. That was nothing like what the real Angrboda could do. Some people believed her, but a good bit of them didn't.

"If they didn't, Thorunn and her followers would slaughter everyone there. They would leave one person alive to spread the word Angrboda killed them for not believing. Most everyone knew she wasn't Angrboda, and anyone she left alive told people a total psychopath was killing people."

That sounded about right. I saw she would become unhinged and dangerous, but I didn't see everything. I saw she would take this total obsession with Angrboda way too far, but I couldn't imagine this.

Ravyn leaned forward and put her elbows on her knees.

"The way conspiracy theory nuts are out and proud now, they'd eat that shit up. Bjorn, did you see how she plans on returning?"

"I saw Asfrid writing a spell in their grimoire, but that's about it."

Killian started nodding.

"Loki said Thorunn wasn't the best spell writer. She must have relied on Asfrid. I'm guessing she kept the grimoire safe since Asfrid was the one writing most of the spells. Would Asfrid have kept the location a secret after they died?"

"If anyone would have, it would have been Asfrid," Sleipnir said. "She was always the nicest to me out of all of them."

"I agree," Loki said. "She was brilliant, but she let Thorunn bully her. I told Asfrid several times that she was stronger than Thorunn and to stand up to her. It wouldn't surprise me if she did that in death."

I always liked Asfrid. She was very sweet, but she was also a total doormat. Loki, Sleipnir, and I all tried to talk her up. If she refused to tell Thorunn the location of the grimoire in death, I was so proud of her.

I felt a pounding behind my eyes. Then, the black spots started swirling, which meant a vision was coming. My body went rigid, and I gasped. Loki caught me as I nearly fell off the sofa. I saw something that terrified me.

Loki and Ravyn both had their arms wrapped around me when I came to.

"Are you okay? That seemed terrible," Ravyn said.

"What did you see?" Loki asked.

"A wolf, standing over a chest full of bones. He's talking to Thorunn's spirit, and she's guiding him. They are both angry. They have Asfrid's spirit there as a hostage."

"That utter mingebag!" Loki yelled. "*That* was why he was stalling me doing the rites. He was collecting the bits of Thorunn and Asfrid like a good little pet. Does he not see the irony of a werewolf hoarding hybrid bones? The spirits fought me, but I didn't see Thorunn's ghost. I didn't question it at the time because she's always been more about letting other people fight her battles. I *hate* being tricked. She's probably been spying on us at the museum!"

"I can say for certain she hasn't," Ravyn said. "My museum is haunted as fuck, but they don't like it if new ghosts show up. There's this entire adjustment period and a lot of bitching if we get a new haunted object. The regular spirits would have made themselves known and demanded answers if Thorunn's ghost was anywhere on the property."

"Asfrid betrayed me like the rest of them, but she doesn't deserve this. Thorunn is only using her for the grimoire and to write more spells. I wish this weren't the type of century where people tend to get upset when you bust up into an inn, kill the bad guy, and make a mess performing rites on some dusty bones."

Ravyn cocked an eyebrow at him.

"So, I'm guessing you weren't joking before about getting arrested?"

"Is that a deal breaker?"

"No. I guess none of this is. I wish you would have trusted us with the truth *before* you kissed either of us, but witches don't fuck with fate. I can't exactly argue with you barging onto Valentine's dig, him picking my museum to bring it to, and your boy seeing me in a vision while he was stuck in a puzzle box. That's fucked up, by the way."

"We majored in fucked up at the academy, Ravyn. How do we fix this?" Killian said.

"We kill him," Sleipnir said.

"I'm not trying to be weird about you being a horse shifter, but hold your damned horses, dude," Ravyn said. "I *am not* getting fired killing a famous archaeologist who has a history with this museum. I did a whole thing in Hell with a pretty famous dragon in the Paranormal Investigation Bureau, and I'm pretty sure he wouldn't throw my ass in jail, but Gertrude, the chairman of the museum board, has a giant stick up her ass."

"Gertrude is terrible, but so is Valentine. I haven't forgotten what you were like after he sent you that book he wrote about all the times he cheated on you. He's gone beyond that now. He's attacking your museum. Valentine is listening to a deranged bear witch who we all know wants to come back and make another cult. We probably won't get out of this without killing *someone,* and you know you want to with Valentine."

This century was so strange. Someone already would have taken care of this wolf for hurting a beautiful woman back in my day. It would have been a toss-up if it were her or someone who cared for her. This century seemed to have a lot of comforts mine didn't, but the asshole population must be raging if there were that many consequences for ridding the world of one. Sleipnir was with me on this.

"Mother, this man hurt your woman, and he's working with the hybrid who betrayed you. Why is he still alive?"

"Good question. I was using the bastard to find out what Thorunn told him about how she planned to return, but he tricked me, and I don't like it."

Of course, he didn't. Loki had tricked most of the gods

more than once. He'd probably fucked a few mortals over now that he wasn't associating with his friends anymore. Loki didn't even think twice about it when he did it to other people. He didn't get tricked often. I'd never personally seen it.

"Okay, it's not a deal breaker that you've been arrested and lied to me. It's even sexy as fuck that you're Loki. If you mess up *anything* in my museum, get me investigated by the Paranormal Investigation Bureau, and Gertrude Von Stein descends on my ass with that terrible old lady perfume micro-managing my museum, *that* is a deal breaker."

"Ravyn, please. I can totally kill a werewolf without doing any of that. You've never seen me in action. I just need to think and plan. I need a good sleep and to watch my enemy more closely. I'll be watching and plotting that asshole's demise when we're back at the museum in the morning."

"How are we going to explain Sleipnir and Bjorn to Valentine?" Killian said.

"Reyson told Ripley the possibilities about my love life. These two pop out of a fucking puzzle box and seem to know me. I don't need to be a god or a seer to see where this is going. We can tell him I brought them in as consultants, but he's always waiting when we get there. When he sees us show up together, he's just going to pitch another fit because he thinks we're dating.

"And I just want to say that if this is a fate thing, it's happening on *my* terms. You're both deathly hot, and I'm curious about the whole hung like a horse thing, but neither of you are going here until you've been properly vetted," she said, pointing to her vagina.

It didn't really make sense to me because my experiences around other supernaturals were limited, but I'd *seen* us all happy together and told Sleipnir as much to give him hope. Sleipnir let out this scandalized gasp, and I knew damned well he loved the company of pretty women. Sometimes more than one pretty woman at once.

"But you're with my mother!"

Loki just shrugged and smirked.

"And we're both with Killian. It's a witch thing that I *fully* support."

Sleipnir looked down at his crotch.

"You're not getting with *this* until I'm okay with this arrangement."

Horses were generally stubborn, and so was Loki. Sleipnir had it on both sides. He'd see. I'd seen plenty of snippets of the battle to come, but not the full picture. I hadn't actually *seen* us win. We didn't have all the answers, and Thorunn had centuries to plan this. I *saw* Thorunn returning at an eclipse. I didn't realize it would take this long for it to happen again.

We had an excellent team, though. We *could* stop this.

Ravyn

My twin had just gone through some crazy shit. We shared everything growing up, and I still had some of her clothes in my closet I needed to bring back now that they were clean. But I didn't want to share the crazy shit. I would officially like to cancel my subscription. Was there a manager I could speak to?

There were only a few people I could tolerate living with, and that was generally Ripley and my parents until Killian got his body back. Loki just fit right in. I already enjoyed giving Sleipnir a hard time, and Bjorn seemed cool, but I *really* hoped they adapted to my cottage that had been updated a lot before I moved in. Mainly not pissing all over my bathrooms and cleaning up after themselves.

I *should* have sent Loki to the doghouse and made him sleep in one of the guest rooms for lying to me, but I didn't. He could have told us the truth. I'm not sure how I could have reacted, but better than finding out he lied to me. I poked him in the chest as soon as we got back to my bedroom.

"I'm still mad you lied."

Loki yanked Killian and me into this massive bear hug.

Why did he have to be such a good hugger when I was trying to be mad at him? He was fighting dirty, and he smelled good too.

"I'm sorry. I know this doesn't mean much coming from Loki, but I'll never lie to you again."

"Do you believe him? Because I do," Killian said.

"Yeah, I do."

"Now that my secret is out of the bag, can I get Killian's?"

I backed them all up until we crashed on my bed. I was smashed between my familiar and a god. It was kind of nice.

"So, my sister's familiar is a cat. When Reyson came back, he was really into Oreos. Felix has several cat traits. He knocked over Reyson's cookies. Felix was an all black cat, and Reyson put white fur on his face in the shape of a dick."

Loki started giggling.

"That checks out with what I know of Reyson. He loves a good dick joke."

"Felix was upset, and Ripley demanded he change it back. Now, as soon as they tricked my twin into bringing Reyson back from the Aether, he pretty much told her they were getting married, even though she was pissed she got tricked and didn't even know him."

"Also, accurate. He's always wanted a mate but never seemed to meet him or her. He probably jumped on it and made a proper ass of himself as soon as he met her."

"Anyway, he thought Felix's dick face was hilarious and wanted to keep it, but my sister wasn't on the god train yet and was mad about it. Reyson didn't want Ripley mad about it, so he just gave Felix his body back in his prime. He offered to do the same for Killian when we were over for dinner trying to figure out the whole Dorian Gray thing. Killian wanted it, and here we are."

"It's a little taboo that you are both with your familiars. I love it."

"It's a little fucked up we both ended up with gods."

Loki kissed the tip of my nose.

"Why? You're both brilliant, powerful Gemini twins. I get you fell for Valentine the first time he was here but be honest with yourself. You would have gotten bored with him eventually, and we see how he takes rejection. He probably would have gotten gross about it, and it would have moved into restraining order territory."

"He's right," Killian said. "I don't even think you *liked* Valentine. Gertrude declined your vacation request when we were going to hit up some ruins in Ireland because Valentine was coming. She also wouldn't let you take a vacation the year before that. So I think you just liked the idea of traveling around and finding the relics yourself because Gertrude is a fucking terrorist with everyone's vacation time, and Valentine was just there."

"You sexy fucker, you're totally right."

Why hadn't I seen that before? I ran the museum and handled all the dangerous relics. I *should* have been able to take a vacation when I wanted and approve it for my employees with no problem. The board shouldn't have been involved in the museum's daily operations at all.

Gertrude Von Stein hated me and everything I stood for. She wasn't chairman of the museum board when I got hired, or she would have made damned sure I never got this job. Gertrude couldn't get rid of me without a unanimous vote from the rest of the board, but she sure as shit like to make my life difficult.

"Who is this Gertrude woman? It's the second time you've mentioned her."

"She's this prudish dragon shifter from a famous line who is now the chairman of the museum board. Gertrude hates witches and thinks we are all sluts. She thinks I'm extra slutty because I don't cover everything but my face in clothes."

"I'd love to meet that one. She'll *hate* me. If she thinks witches are sluts, you pretty much have nothing on gods. We invented orgies. Slut shaming is stupid anyway. Like, don't get mad at *me* because no one wants to fuck you."

"Thank you! She's from one of those wealthy families that arranges marriages. Her husband is something like her seventh cousin, and they can't stand each other. The reason she hates me is that the board threw this big gala for a new exhibit and invited everyone interviewing for my job. Her crusty ass husband, who has never heard of trimming his nose hair, cornered me by the canapes and told me he could get me the job for sure if I fucked him."

"I'm guessing that didn't end well for him?"

Killian started laughing.

"Ravyn smashed a crab Rangoon in his face and cursed his dick. The rest of the board was pretty impressed with the magic Ravyn used. Gertrude wasn't amused and blamed Ravyn for fighting back instead of her husband, who had it coming."

"I'm guessing you refused to remove the curse too."

I started laughing at the memory, and the time I got to stick it to Gertrude Von Stein.

"That's the thing with witch curses. There's this beautiful solidarity in the witching community. No one is going to remove another witch's curse without asking what you did to earn it. My twin is shacking up with a vampire who applied for his library card to try to get rid of a curse on his cock. No one would remove it, but Ripley and I went to the Academy of the Profane with the witch who did it. She got expelled because she'd get infatuated with someone, aggressively stalk them, then leave them with a really complicated curse on their junk. It took Ripley two tries to get it off Balthazar's."

"So, what happened with that?"

"Well, Gertrude demanded I be disqualified from the

hiring process, but I was the only applicant who had a personal letter of recommendation from Minerva Krauss that I spent three years doing independent study with her at the Academy of the Profane, and she was still mentoring me after I graduated. That trumps one pissed off dragon and her husband with a cursed dick."

"Everyone on the board wanted Ravyn except Gertrude. She was outvoted and couldn't do a damn thing to stop it. Her condition for supporting it was that she remove the curse. His ancient dick probably only works with the help of a pill he gets from a doctor. She should have been *thanking* Ravyn. If a witch her age took him up on that, he'd die during foreplay, and just think of the scandal! Ravyn did her a favor taking his cock out of commission."

I just adored Killian. He had my back on everything. So did Loki, apparently.

"I can set this Gertrude straight," Loki said.

"We need to be less worried about Gertrude Von Stein and more worried about Valentine and the ghosts who are whispering to him."

That was an excellent point. Bringing Thorunn's bones here and keeping Asfrid hostage explained why his aura kept darkening, and he was giving me the creeps. Now, I *really* didn't want him in my presence. Why were we even talking about my dragon nemesis instead of Valentine and his ghosts?

"I'm changing tactics," Loki said. "I just need a good sleep snuggled up to people I care about, secure in the knowledge that Sleipnir and Bjorn are with me again. I'll get answers out of him at the warehouse, and then we'll move."

"He's not going to talk to you, dude. You clocked the shite out of him, and then we all left him in the rain," Killian said.

"I spoke to him in a language he understands. He's not an alpha, even though he likes to claim he is. Valentine is a wolf without a pack. They banished him from his, and if he wanted to join another one, he'd have to fight. I asserted dominance. He can challenge me or move on. He doesn't *know* I'm a god, but he knows I'm powerful. He won't fight me."

"That doesn't mean he's going to cooperate. He likes to sulk."

"Hello? I'm Loki. I'll get it out of him."

I only hoped it was that easy because the eclipse was rapidly approaching.

CHAPTER 37

Loki

Ravyn liked her sleep. She had that in common with Bjorn. I snuck out of bed with Killian to make sure we had breakfast prepared for the two sleepyheads. I knew Sleipnir would be awake. I wanted to show him the modern world. He wasn't in his bedroom, so I went to the front of the house. I saw him in the gardens outside the window.

Oh, no. Oh, fuck no. I went running out there. Ravyn was going to have a stroke.

"No pissing in a witch's herb garden, son!" I yelled.

Oh, shit. Sleipnir finished pissing, shook himself off, and stuck his cock back in his trousers. He emptied his bladder all over her lavender, and I knew she probably used that a lot.

"Where else am I supposed to piss? I have to take a shit too. That was a lot of food last night."

If he took a cheeseburger shit in her yard, Ravyn was going to flip. I should have shown him the toilets before we went to bed. I was a terrible mother.

"They have indoor plumbing in this century. Right this way."

I led Sleipnir inside. Killian saw the whole thing. He was glaring at us with his arms crossed. Could I bribe him to keep this a secret from Ravyn? My son pissed all over her lavender, and I didn't want her to hold it against him.

"You'd better potty train your son, Loki," Killian said.

I scowled at him and led Sleipnir to the bathroom. He was potty trained. He'd just never seen a modern toilet before. I pointed at it.

"You piss and shit in that. Then, you use the toilet paper on the wall to wipe your ass. Hit that lever when you're done, and it'll disappear. Don't use too much toilet paper, or you'll clog the toilet and flood the bathroom."

"I get it. Do you mind?"

I left Sleipnir to do his business. He was a smart lad. I would only need to tell him once. It wasn't his fault he was new to this century.

Sleipnir was safe. Sometime in the seventies, I went to one of Odin's book signings. We went out for a few beers afterwards and rehashed everything. We were good now. He got what he did to me and why I went after his son. He wasn't looking for Sleipnir. The only reason I hadn't let him out was because of the eclipse.

Odin wasn't *bad*. He was mostly pretty cool. He was just scared of me. Odin sacrificed a lot for his knowledge, but even with all of it, he could never figure out what I was going to do next. If Sleipnir had just been a regular horse, he would have been spoiled rotten. Odin had a whole menagerie of animals that were all treated very well.

But Sleipnir wasn't an ordinary horse. Yes, he loved shifting and running, but my boy also craved the company of people. So, I really didn't want Ravyn upset with him because he pissed in her garden. Odin promised to leave him alone and even said he would apologize to my son if he ever saw him again.

The only people Sleipnir and Bjorn were in danger from now were Thorunn and Valentine. I had to believe Asfrid's ghost was there against her will. I don't think any god told anyone to sacrifice anything to them, but back in the day, they did it anyway. Thorunn knew that damn well. I told her multiple times.

It was annoying she never listened, and then she got this grand idea that it would impress me to sacrifice my son. All of this was some fucked up attempt to impress me. She wanted to be my wife and rule by my side. At least, that was how it started. After that, I think she just enjoyed reveling in her evilness. Some people just ended up wrong.

When I went back to the kitchen, Killian was cooking and dancing to music on his cell phone. I gave his backside a little spank. He was just so adorable in appearance but hiding so much power. Valentine was much bigger than he was, but Killian easily kicked his ass. He had to be a powerful warlock to be paired up with Ravyn as her familiar.

"I will give you whatever the fuck you want if you don't mention that little incident in the garden to Ravyn."

"Are you kidding? She's going to find that *hilarious*. No one has pissed in her plants before. If it had been one of the potted ones inside, she'd be furious. Outside? She's going to laugh about it."

"At Sleipnir's expense. He didn't know better. Sleipnir is highly intelligent but spent his formative years as a horse. Thorunn was jealous of all the time I spent with him adapting to life on two legs. He said nothing to me, and Sleipnir would never hit a woman, but she said terrible things to him. Sleipnir ignored her because that's just who he is, but Bjorn insulted her right back.

"Sleipnir asked Bjorn not to tell me. Those two aren't related in the traditional sense, but they became blood brothers like Odin and me. Bjorn kept his secret until he came to me with the vision I would get caught, and Thorunn was going to fuck off and get dangerous. I owe Thorunn for every terrible thing she said to my boy, but I *really* like Ravyn and you too. I get the whole flirting thing she's doing with him, but I don't want it to get ugly."

"Oh, she wouldn't be making fun of him, and neither am I. Back when Ravyn and Ripley were at the Academy of the Profane, this pack of rich werewolves was there. They'd tell anyone who would listen they could trace their line to the original wolf pack Selene created. Anyway, they grew up around toilets but didn't believe in them."

I frowned because that didn't make any type of sense.

"A toilet isn't Santa Claus or the Easter Bunny. There are literally multiple toilets in every building and household. So how does one *not* believe in toilets?"

I'd been alive a long time. I'd seen people believe in some crazy shit. I'd seen people whip up elaborate conspiracy theories because the truth made them uncomfortable. Conspiracy theories seemed to abound lately, and those people were so much fun to trick. So I infiltrated all their safe spaces and made up all kinds of crazy stories for shits and giggles.

I was doing a science project. Exactly how ridiculous could I get before it was unbelievable to these people? So far, the limit did not exist. I'd never once tried to make up a conspiracy theory to get people to stop using toilets. But, I couldn't take credit for this one, and I wanted to know more.

"Okay, so this pack thought shitting and pissing in their wolf form was superior to toilets. Hell, maybe it is. I'm not exactly a werewolf to test that theory. The professors hated it when they had to leave class to go to the restroom because they had to go outside, get naked, shift, and find the right spot.

"The other wolves thought they were insane, and this particular wolf pack thought they were just low class for not pooping in nature. So anyway, students were stepping in it in the common areas. The professors hated it, and so did the board at the academy, but they didn't tell them to stop because they didn't want to be accused of being insensitive to shifters. So, they roped off a designated pooping area where they could shit. I'm sure plenty of the other shifters took a crap outside when they were outside enjoying their beasts, but when they were walking on two legs, they preferred indoor plumbing."

I started laughing. I could appreciate when things got fucked up on their own, and I didn't have a hand in it. I so needed to make that a thing. I didn't want my son taking a shit outside, but it would be fucking *hilarious* if I tricked other people into doing it.

I was going to make it a thing when this was over.

"Okay, I get why you would find that hilarious, but please, don't rope my son into that nonsense. He—"

Just then, Sleipnir joined us in the kitchen to prove my point.

"I wish we had those in the pocket realm. This century is exciting. How are you cooking without fire?" he demanded.

"Okay, he's adorable," Killian said. "This is a stove. That right there is a microwave. You can cook things in that too. Over there is the fridge. You put food in there to keep it cold and from spoiling. You put things in the freezer if you buy something but don't want to cook it right away. There's also ice cream in there, but best buy your own because Ravyn will murder you if you eat her Chunky Monkey. Where is Bjorn? He should be here for this."

"Where's Ravyn?" Sleipnir asked. "Aren't we going to battle?"

"Not just yet. I need to learn my enemy's weaknesses. Ravyn and Bjorn have some things in common. Neither of them like waking up in the morning."

"So, I have breakfast waiting so she can eat when she gets

to work. If you have the option to spoil Ravyn, you should always take it,"

"What about my mother?" Sleipnir said. "He's a god!"

"Who hates having a fuss made about him. I spoil her too, Sleipnir. It's what you do when you care about someone, no matter how powerful you are."

"I cooked for you and Bjorn too, and I just met you. See? I can spoil you too."

"Thanks. Sorry, I'm still getting used to all this and being around more people than just Bjorn again."

"Ravyn and I will help. We're going to have to take you and Bjorn shopping. You can pick out clothes you like and bath products."

"Deodorant is a beautiful thing about this century. We'll get you some. I'm immortal, but I *swear* by this moisturizer made by the Seelie. We'll all get you set up in the modern world."

"We just have to beat Valentine and his ghosts first," Killian said.

"Yeah, but I have a plan for that," I said.

I just needed to look Valentine in the eye and ask him a few questions to figure out what that plan was.

CHAPTER 38

Ravyn

Bjorn stumbled out of his bedroom right around the time I did. He grinned when he saw me like he knew something I didn't. He probably did. That bitch saw the future.

"Don't worry. I found the toilet okay and figured out how to use it," he said with a smirk.

"Why? Did someone not?"

Someone better not have pissed in my house.

"Your house is clean, Ravyn. I think your men prepared breakfast."

"Have you seen anything new?" I asked.

"Not since last night. I don't really have control over my visions. I tried to learn it while we were in the pocket realm, but I can't force it. I can't stop it when it's happening either. It just is."

I felt bad for him. I used to think I wanted the power to see the future, but then I met Bjorn and saw him have a vision.

"It seems painful."

"It's tiring and can be painful while it's coming on, but once I sleep, I'm fine."

"I have some recipes that might help you. I'm not sure. They help replenish magic for witches if they use too much. You aren't exactly a witch, but it couldn't hurt," I said as we walked into the kitchen.

Maybe those awful cooking lessons with Old Scratch would pay off if it would help Bjorn. Killian and Loki didn't do all the cooking. Yeah, we got delivery, but they did breakfast and I made dinner for the most part. I usually packed leftovers or made sandwiches for lunch at work.

When I got to the kitchen, Killian and Loki were packing up breakfast, and Sleipnir had his head in my fridge. What was he doing? He shut the door when he realized Bjorn and I were here and grinned at me.

"That's amazing! You can keep your food cold when it isn't winter, and you don't have to eat the meat or salt it immediately!"

Okay, Sleipnir was the cutest thing I'd ever seen. He was pretty much the same height as Loki but more muscular. Sleipnir looked like he could rip a bitch in half if he wanted to. He was losing his shit over my fridge. Oh, I was going to have so much fun showing this one everything about this century.

Bjorn wouldn't have known what any of this was either, but he seemed to just take everything in and adapt. I appreciated that about him. Killian had his hands full trying to rein me in, and I had a feeling Loki and I were going to feed off of each other. Bjorn could be an additional sane person to our group because that certainly wasn't Loki or me.

I could have been mad Loki sprung additional houseguests on me, but I wasn't. I could have asked them all to go back to the hotel, but I didn't want to. They were a part of this. They could help us stop Valentine and Thorunn.

I didn't know if this was some fucked up fate thing like my sister had with the library cards. I didn't *want* to think about it, so I wasn't. I was just going to take things as they came. Fate might have opinions about my love life, but so did I. I seemed to be hitting the cock lottery right after I ended my dick exile, but I wasn't rushing into anything.

At least, that was what I was telling myself. Unfortunately, fate was a little bitch.

"Wait until I show you movies and the supernatural market, big guy. Welcome to capitalism. It doesn't all suck."

"He was fucked off to the Aether, but capitalism just *screams* Reyson," Loki said. "There are now a million different kinds of breakfast cereals that are twists on the exact same thing, but people can't afford medication. That has God of Chaos all over it, but Reyson wouldn't have done that."

"I'm so confused," Sleipnir said.

I wrapped my arm around his waist. At least, I tried to. Wow, he was big and firm. I wanted to show him everything because there was this genuine joy in him at seeing new things, but I didn't want to overwhelm Sleipnir. I wanted him to like this century and fit right in because it meant a lot to Loki.

"Baby steps. You don't have to see everything at once. How about you come see where I work first? It's a pretty famous museum. We have items and relics from all over the world. We can give you a tour and a history lesson of some of the things that happened while you were gone."

"I'd like that too," Bjorn said.

Sleipnir frowned.

"Did you plunder so many villages that people pay you to come to see the treasure you stole?"

I started choking because that was a sensitive topic for literally everyone at the Museum of the Profane. I got why Sleipnir said that. There weren't museums around back in his day, but we were a different kind of museum.

Nothing in here was stolen from any culture. If we got something we suspected should be with a group that was currently still alive and might want it, we reached out to them about returning their historical items. This wouldn't have been my dream job since I was in high school if this museum were like some of the other museums and put things on display that had significance to living people.

Estates donated everything here, or when asked, the people in the area didn't want it. Sometimes, things were discovered that were considered bad luck or dangerous to the locals. Those all came to me to diffuse and then go on display. Sometimes, famous people died and were estranged from their families. They didn't want them getting a damned thing when they died.

They'd keep it this big secret, and when their family would go to the will reading after expecting money and property, they'd find out they were fucked. Most of the time, all the money was split between the Academy, Museum, and Library of the Profane. They split everything in the house. Books went to the library, and magical and historical items came to the museum. There was generally an additional fuck you in there that their houses and other properties were donated to organizations that would put them to good use.

So, yeah. Sleipnir was used to Vikings, and I got why he said that but we put a *lot* of care at my museum to have banging exhibits that people came from everywhere to see, but *not* stealing things from cultures that wanted the items. How did I explain this to him?

"All the items were given to us. If they were brought to us, but they belonged to someone else, we gave them back."

Sleipnir's eyes widened, and he looked at me in awe.

"Are you a queen? I'm sorry, I didn't know."

Oh, my Lilith, I really wanted to hug him. Was that weird? This big, massive man with hair plenty of people paid good money to try to get at the salon was looking at me like I was an actual queen because I ran a museum. How adorable was that?

I just went for it. I wrapped my arms around him and

squeezed him. And I made him totally uncomfortable. It was either a Loki thing or the fact that he still thought I was a queen.

"I'm not even remotely close to a queen, Sleipnir. Most places don't have kings and queens anymore, but a few do. I'm not remotely responsible for laws being made. I try to be by voting, but sometimes, politicians promise shit when they are running and then don't follow through when they are elected. I can't even approve vacation time because Gertrude is a frigid, slut shaming toad who hates me."

"Do you want us to kill this Gertrude? Why are you hugging me?"

"You can't kill people in this century because they are irritating, but it means a lot that you offered. I hugged you because you're just so precious."

Sleipnir grunted.

"I can run between realms when I'm shifted and kill a man with my bare hands."

"I know. You could probably snap me in half if you wanted to. But, I still think you're cute."

"Take the compliment and the hug, son. We should get to the museum. Valentine will be waiting, and that eclipse isn't going to wait for any of us. I *need* to ask him the right questions this time."

"Do you actually *know* what those questions are?" Killian asked. "You've been pretty vague."

"I'll know when I look him in the eyes."

Oh, my Lilith. I was hoping to play the whole god get out of jail free card when it came to stopping the Cult of the Aether Sisters from returning, and he was just pantsing his way through this.

The eclipse was in five days, and Loki didn't actually know what the fuck he was doing.

CHAPTER 39

Ravyn

We walked over to the museum in silence. I was basically too pretty to survive without electricity and deodorant, but I kind of wished things were like what they were before Sleipnir and Bjorn went into that box. We could just show up at the warehouse, kill Valentine, and then go fetch the bones for Loki to do the rites.

The law tended to frown on killing people nowadays, even if they cheated on you and then bought ghosts back with them to raise a deranged cult leader. Should I call Kaine? I got his number the first time we met Beyla. Could that grumpy dragon even do anything since he hadn't broken the law? Was keeping crusty ass bones in your hotel room and bringing ghosts to an otherwise unhaunted hotel against the law?

All of that was moot. All this time, every time we got to the warehouse, Valentine was skulking outside, waiting to be let in because I refused to get him a key. I could have easily had one made for him, but I didn't. Even after what he did to me, I would have, but his aura frankly creeped me out. After I found out what he got up to on that dig, there was no way in shit I was giving him the keys to my kingdom.

"What now?" I asked.

Loki's entire plan involved asking him questions in the warehouse. Valentine had been here without fail every morning. He was the type to hold epic grudges, and technically Killian and Loki had both kicked his ass. I was guilty by association because I left him in the rain. Maybe he'd finally gotten it through his thick skull I wasn't going back there.

Still, Thorunn was a master manipulator if she got everyone to betray Loki like that. She formed a cult before there was even a word for it. Valentine was in her thrall enough to steal her bones before the rites could be performed and take Asfrid too because she wanted it.

"Give me a minute," Loki said.

I was learning all gods had unique powers. I was guessing Loki could put himself in a trance like Reyson and Lilith did to visit the hotel and see if Valentine were there astrally. I also knew he was super pissed about getting tricked and would want to go in person.

He was definitely going to make a mess at the hotel, but I watched Reyson explode Dorian Gray in a cloud of pink glitter just to stick it to Felix, and I was guessing Loki knew his way around disposing of bodies. I mean, he wouldn't *technically* be killing Valentine on the museum grounds, so there wouldn't be some random wolf DNA hiding in a crack somewhere when his fangirl Gertrude reported him missing and blamed me.

Reyson always disappeared in a pop of light. Lilith conjured doors out of thin air. Loki disappeared in a big flash of flame and left us all outside the warehouse holding our dicks. Sleipnir was sulking.

"I *hate* when he does that and doesn't take me."

"Best not let Thorunn's ghost know you're walking the Earth again just yet," Killian said.

"Why don't you all step into my office?"

I let them into the warehouse. We didn't just have things from the Cult of the Aether Sisters here. There were plenty of other relics in here that I was trying to figure out how to diffuse. Some of them, I didn't exactly know what was wrong with them. If someone dug them up and locals didn't want them, there was generally something fucked up about it.

Sleipnir went straight to the giant bronze horse we got from China. The thing was massive and gorgeous. *Someone* would have wanted to keep it unless something was wrong with it. Sleipnir looked like he was about to touch it.

It was like slow motion. I wasn't close enough to stop him, but Killian was. Killian took off running and tried to tackle Sleipnir, who might as well have been made of bronze like that fucking horse. Killian just kind of bounced off him, but Sleipnir lowered his hand and wasn't trying to touch it anymore.

"Why did you assault me, warlock?"

"Almost everything in here is dangerous to touch unless you know what you're doing."

"But this horse is already dead. What did they do to it?"

Adorable. The bronze horse was well done and extremely lifelike. I could see where the confusion came from.

"This is metal. I'm pretty sure no horses were harmed in the making of this statue, but I'm not completely sure. The zodiac is different where this horse comes from. The horse is a star sign, so it's represented a lot in art. Someone in Macau initially claimed it when we put out feelers. Two weeks later, they called us, begging us to take it from them.

"Apparently, if you touch it, all your money tends to disappear. I haven't figured out how to disable it, but I've researched it. It was made as a birthday gift for an emperor who was born under the sign of the horse. I'm guessing he was a greedy shit bag to be given something like this. Anyway, you shouldn't touch it. You don't even have a bank account, so I can't imagine what it would take from you."

Loki appeared again in a puff of fire. He looked pretty pissed.

"Valentine and the bones are no longer at the hotel room. The front desk said he checked out yesterday."

"He's not gone," Killian said. "He still needs the grimoire."

"Unless they've forced Asfrid to write a new spell," Loki said.

"They still need a witch," I pointed out.

"Maybe they don't," Bjorn said. "The hybrids were dual natured. Eclipses had all kinds of power for the shifters back in our day. Asfrid could have written a spell for a shifter, and that was why they waited this entire time."

I didn't like that. I didn't like that at all. I liked it even less when Sasha came stumbling into the warehouse holding her head, and there was blood running down her forehead.

"I thought that bloody werewolf was supposed to be on our side? He knocked on my door. I know you said not to let him in, but he attacked me. He ripped a page out of the grimoire and ran."

Shit. *Shit!* No one had ever stolen from the Museum of the Profane before, much less a contractor who came highly recommended by the board. Who was I supposed to call for this? Gertrude would want to know since Valentine was only here because of her. If I was going to have the Paranormal Investigation Bureau here, I wanted Kaine.

I also really wanted to call my twin.

This had honestly never happened to me before. The museum hadn't been robbed. *Why* did it have to happen on my watch? No, I needed to think about my employee. I helped Sasha over to a chair.

"How are you?"

"Fucker hit me with a brick, but vampire healing, you know. I got the page he stole scanned before he ripped it out. So I can get it emailed to you."

"You need to go to the hospital."

"Yeah, no. If you're hunting that fucker down, I want in. I'm fine. You need to call Gertrude."

We all looked at each other. Bjorn's theory was probably right. If Valentine stole one page and not the entire grimoire, then there was the possibility a shifter could do their resurrection spell.

And Valentine now had it. Fuck Gertrude. I was calling Kaine, then my twin.

Afterword

Thank you for reading Ravyn's book! I hope you enjoyed it. Book 2 is coming as soon as I wrap up Beyla's series. There is also a spinoff planned with Ripley's twins from The Library of the Profane. I did a cover reveal for those in my reader's group, which you can check out by joining us here.

CPSIA information can be obtained
at www.ICGtesting.com
Printed in the USA
BVHW052002141022
649468BV00005B/847